Father Roberto and the Rural Riots

Two heartwarming cosy mysteries

Stefania Hartley

THE·SICILIAN·MAMA

To Robert Maxwell. Thank you for your wonderful friendship and encouragement.

CONTENTS

1 The Rural Riots   1

2 The Stolen Statue   78

   Other Books by the Author   121

   About the Author   123

1. THE RURAL RIOTS

Chapter 1

Father Roberto loved spending his annual leave away from Palermo and back to his hometown, in the Sicilian Madonie mountains.

In Vicina everyone knew everyone, and Father Roberto was simply "Roberto", or even "Robertino" for those who had known him as a baby.

But it was especially in his parents' home that he was demoted from "Father" to child.

"Can you run to the baker and get some bread for our lunch?" his mother asked him, despite him being past the age of running in the streets.

Roberto never understood what was wrong with the bread the baker took out of the oven in the morning, and why his parents needed a fresh loaf at lunchtime.

But he obediently put down the Confessions

of Saint Augustine and slipped his feet into his sandals.

Just as he was leaving the house, his mother called from the kitchen to remind him to take a hat because the sun was hot at this time of day.

Roberto put on his straw hat and set off. The sun was indeed very hot—just as he remembered from his childhood and youth. In fact, the whole town was just as he remembered it, which was a very comforting thing. It made him feel that he hadn't missed out on anything.

He hadn't walked more than twenty metres when he saw Nonna Maria. She wasn't Roberto's grandma—or anyone else's, for that matter—but the whole town called her 'nonna' out of respect for her age. But despite her age and unsteady legs, she was carrying a chair down the street.

Roberto rushed to help.

"Hello, Nonna Maria. Can I carry this for you?"

"You're not a priest. You're an angel!" she told him with a smile that brought out a range of friendly wrinkles.

"Where are you going to?"

"To the woods, of course."

He had never seen her leave her house other

than to go to church. What could she possibly be doing in the woods in the hottest part of the day?

"Are you sure you want to go there?" Roberto asked her gently, as doubts about her sanity flitted across his mind.

"Absolutely! I can't be the only one missing," she replied with determination.

Roberto concluded that she must have lost her sanity. But as he glanced around for help, he saw the butcher's mother step out of her door with a chair and nod at Nonna Maria. Further down the road, another woman stood by her door with a folding chair under one arm and her knitting under the other.

"What's happening in the woods?" Roberto asked Nonna Maria.

She stopped and looked at him with surprise. "Haven't your parents told you?"

"About what?"

Nonna Maria shook her head in disapproval. "The mayor has given permission to build a road across the woods."

"How could he do that? Some of the trees are very old or rare species," Roberto objected.

"That's what we all say. This is why the women of Vicina are going to sit in the woods in protest, twenty-four-seven."

This explained why all Vicina's women were

pouring into the town's main street with all kinds of chairs—from wicker chairs to camping stools—headed for the woods.

A sea of green canopies lined the side of the mountain and the valley below Vicina, swishing and swooshing with the ebb and flow of the wind. It was mainly broadleaves—hazels, beech, oak and ash—but a few fir trees dotted the landscape with their darker foliage, sticking out straight like lances to snag passing clouds.

With its shape and orientation, the valley trapped moist air rising from the sea, glittering in the distance, and kept it green and lush even during the summer months, when the rest of Sicily turned into dry scrubland. All this made Vicina's woods an almost magical place.

The meeting place was under a very special fir tree, the *Abies nebrodensis*. The Sicilian fir grew only in these mountains and this was the only remaining tree. Its value was immeasurable.

At the sight of the magnificent ancient tree, Roberto felt an ache in the back of his throat. It was under its branches that he had first heard the call to the priesthood on a spring evening when the air sparkled with light and possibilities.

It was here that he had often come to be alone, think or just admire God's handiwork.

When his future was still a mystery and his place in the world not guaranteed, he had come here to let the song of the wind through the leaves soothe his soul.

But now the place was completely different, buzzing with activity and chatter. The women sat on scuffed plastic chairs, smart dining chairs, or sporty folding chairs and chatted while they knitted, crocheted and embroidered. With coffee pots gurgling on camping stoves and trays of baked goods, everyone seemed set to have a very good time.

The baked goods reminded Roberto that he should have already been home with the bread by now.

He said goodbye to Nonna Maria and ran to the bakery only to find it already shut. So he walked back home, dreading the moment he'd tell his mum that there was no fresh bread for their lunch.

Chapter 2

When Roberto got home—late and breadless—his mother welcomed him with a beaming smile.

"Your brother is coming tomorrow! I'll have both my boys here!" she told Roberto excitedly.

Roberto's relief at not being told off about the bread was dampened by the news.

He had looked forward to spending his time at home in peace and quiet. Now that his elder brother was coming home there would be tension, competition and put downs.

Roberto had a feeling that Corrado had never got over the end of his only-childhood, and that he still resented Roberto for it.

"I'll sleep on the sofa," Roberto volunteered.

"You don't have to. I'm sure Corrado wouldn't mind sharing his room with you, like in the old times," his mother said.

Roberto notice that she still considered their shared bedroom Corrado's room.

The room had started off as Corrado's bedroom before Roberto was born, then the two of them had shared it, but his parents had continued to consider it Corrado's room. Even when Corrado had left home and Roberto became its sole occupant, he never stopped feeling like a guest in his brother's room. It looked like this holiday was going to be no exception.

Feeling in need of distraction before his brother's arrival, Roberto organised to meet up with his childhood friends that evening.

Vicina didn't have a nightlife as such, but some cafés had started opening late into the evening, and Roberto met up with his friends at one of them.

Seeing the people he had grown up with gave Roberto a swell of warmth and happiness. Many of them were married with children now, but they had made time to meet him, and some of them had even come with their spouses.

Sitting around a table with drinks and cakes, enjoying his friends' company and affection, Roberto thought that Heaven might be a bit like this—enjoying the company of good people who loved you. He couldn't imagine getting bored of it even after an eternity.

After catching up with their news—births, marriages, job changes—Roberto asked them about the new road.

The tone of their conversation immediately changed—all cheerfulness instantly evaporated.

"Yes, they're planning to cut a road through our woods," Sergio confirmed with a gloomy face.

"But why? That's an ancient woodland, and the home of some extremely rare species. Isn't there any other way?"

"Yes, there is an alternative route, but it would go through the land of the Cacciatore family, and they don't want it."

At the mention of the local criminal family, Roberto didn't need any further explanations.

"That's why the women of Vicina have organised a sit-in to protest against the road and to guard the woods against the diggers," Maura added.

"It won't stop the Cacciatore," Sergio said.

"Let's not talk about upsetting things," Arianna interrupted them. "Roberto, tell us what you've been up to since we last saw you."

Roberto hadn't been home for months and plenty of things had happened in the meantime. He could tell his friend about how he had recovered a stolen engagement ring, or about his role in rescuing his kidnapped parish priest. But something else was on his mind.

"Corrado is arriving tomorrow."

"Oh, no. I'm sorry," Sergio replied.

"Why? Corrado adores Roberto," Maura said.

"I wouldn't say that," Sergio objected. "Do you remember when Corrado tried to sell

Roberto to the shepherds?"

Roberto remembered that the shepherds wouldn't buy him even for one lira. It had been a little embarrassing.

"But Corrado always stood up to Roberto's bullies at school," Maura countered.

The fact that Roberto couldn't stand up for himself was also a little embarrassing.

"That's all in the past," Roberto said, suddenly keen to move the conversation on to other topics.

But as he walked back to his parents' flat that night, Roberto thought about Corrado again. Did Corrado love him or hate him? Perhaps both?

After all, Corrado had rushed to his brother's help when Roberto was searching for the stolen ring. Maybe the upcoming days together could be the time when their relationship finally took a permanent turn for the better.

Chapter 3

Out of the window, the sky was a pale pink, the pastel beginning of a new day.

"Thank you, God, for keeping me from sin today," Roberto prayed. "But now you've got to help me more, because I'm about to get out of bed."

Now that early summer had rolled into late summer, sunrise was no longer buried in the early hours of the morning. Roberto would have happily slept for another eight hours, but he had promised the parish priest that he would help him with the confessions.

This effectively turned Roberto's home leave into a busman's holiday, but Father Andrea had been Roberto's parish priest all through his childhood and adolescence. Roberto felt that lending a hand during his visits home was the least he could do to pay Father Andrea back for all he had done for him.

Roberto heaved himself out of bed and padded to the kitchen, where he found his parents discussing something animatedly.

As soon as they saw him, they stopped—just as they had when he was a child.

"Is everything okay?" Roberto asked.

His parents looked at each other, trying to decide to tell him or not.

"They've cut down the tree," his father said.

"Which tree?"

"The one next to the women's sit-in."

"You don't mean the *Abies nebrodensis*, surely?"

"That's the one," his mother confirmed, and showed him a photo of a jagged tree stump on her phone.

Roberto looked closely. Yes, it looked just like someone had badly hacked away at the last specimen of Sicilian fir on earth.

Roberto had mentally prepared for a difficult day due to Corrado's arrival, but this was bad news on a different scale.

The fact that his beloved tree had such a high scientific value had lulled Roberto into believing that nothing bad could ever happen to it. But it just had.

"How could they do it, if the women were sitting under its branches twenty-four-seven?" Roberto asked.

His mother sighed. "Last night was Rosaria Pace's turn. Around midnight, she felt too cold and went home to get a blanket. If you believe her story, she went straight back and found the tree gone, just like that. But if you ask me, when she went home she got into bed and slept there. Then she returned to her post the next morning."

"This is all very suspicious," Roberto's father said, tapping his nose. "That tree formed the main case against the building of the road. Now that it's gone, the environmentalists and the scientists who wanted to block the construction of the road have a much weaker case."

"We all know who's cut the tree down," Roberto's mother said sourly, "but whether they'll ever be punished for it, that's a different matter."

In low spirits, Roberto set off for the church.

With its mixture of Arab-Norman and gothic elements, plus additions from the 18th century, the church witnessed the resilience of the people of Vicina, who had repeatedly rebuilt it after wars and earthquakes.

Roberto stepped out of the hot, dusty street into the cooler church, with its familiar smell of old stones and incense.

Father Andrea looked as subdued as him.

"Thank you for manning the confessional booth while I do my pastoral visits. You should have a quiet time today: the whole town is in mourning for the tree," the elderly priest told him sadly.

"I don't mind helping. It will take my mind off the tree too," Roberto said. "Unless, of course, it's the tree-cutters who come for confession."

Roberto imagined the scene. Would he have enough professional detachment to give them the absolution, or would he leap out of the confessional booth and throttle them? He decided he had better ask God to help him about that.

"Unfortunately, it still wouldn't bring the tree back," Father Andrea said sadly.

The other priest left and Roberto was left alone in the church. Through the beautiful stained-glass window the Sicilian sun streamed onto the pews like the fire of the Holy Spirit.

Roberto knew the picture of every window by heart. This was the church which was more familiar to him than any other.

It was here that, as a child, he had been an altar server—and had often fallen asleep during the early morning Masses. In front of this altar he had received his first Holy Communion. Under this painted-wood crucifix he had prayed fervently for clarity about his vocation to the priesthood, and had received it.

The fir tree where he'd had his first inspiration to become a priest was gone, but the church where his faith and his vocation had grown was still standing and was as beautiful as ever.

Roberto opened the creaky door of the mahogany confessional, sat inside, opened the curtains and settled down to pray with his Divine Office book.

He had only got to the second Psalm when he heard steps on the church's stone floor. A few moments later, the booth's kneeler creaked.

"Hello, Father Roberto," the voice of a woman greeted him through the grille.

"Hello," Roberto greeted her back.

He didn't know who she was: the grille's holes were too small and he didn't recognise her voice.

"They've done a very bad thing to us," the woman began.

"Confession is about repenting of our own sins, not other people's," Roberto reminded her gently.

"I'm not here to confess anything because we haven't done anything—and that is precisely the problem. I'm here to tell you that we're innocent and you must help us."

Roberto started to wonder about the woman's sanity. "I'm sorry, I don't quite understand. Maybe you'd like to come back when Father Andrea is here," Roberto told her gently.

Father Andrea would know who she was

and, perhaps, what she was talking about.

"No, Roberto. We need you," the woman replied forcefully. "We've heard what you've done in Palermo—how you discovered who had stolen the engagement ring; how you helped two rival clans make peace."

Roberto was a little unnerved. Only his closest family and friends knew about the events she was referring to.

"Who are you?" he asked.

"I'm the grandma of the Alessio family."

Roberto recognised that name. They were the Cacciatores' rival criminal clan. Whatever she had come to ask him, it couldn't be good news. Why couldn't he have a normal, restful holiday, like other priests?

"We didn't cut the tree down, I swear."

"We don't swear in church."

"Sorry. What I mean is, I'm telling the truth."

"We must always tell the truth."

"Of course—except when we can't."

Roberto decided it was better to give up on this.

"So, if you didn't cut the tree down, what's your problem?" he asked her.

"The Cacciatores don't believe us. They didn't cut it down either, so they're convinced that we must have done it."

"Why would you do something that would help their cause about the road?" Roberto asked.

"To insult them by acting inside their territory without their permission, and to make everyone believe that they did it. So now they're mad with us and are plotting revenge."

"That's very unfortunate, but I'm not sure how I can help," Roberto told her.

"You must find who did it and tell the Cacciatores."

"Why me? That's a job for the police."

"By the time the police find who did it, someone will have already been killed. And once the Cacciatores murder one of ours, we will have to murder one of theirs. There isn't going to be an end to the killings."

"How about your family refraining from taking revenge? Then the vendetta chain will stop," Roberto suggested.

The woman snorted. "Good luck persuading my son to do that! Nobody wants to be the first one to leave a crime unpunished and look weak. No, Father, you are the only one who can stop this."

Roberto still wasn't convinced. "Why me? I'm sure your family can find out who cut the tree down much more easily than I could ever do."

"Because even if we found the real culprits with the bark of the tree still stuck to their chainsaws, the Cacciatores wouldn't believe us. But they will believe you. If you refuse to help us and the chain of vendettas starts, all the spilled blood will be on your head."

Roberto shuddered at the gruesome thought.

He had come home to rest and recuperate after a year of hard work and stress. The task he was being asked to do didn't sound like rest and recuperation. But even if he refused to take it on, how could he rest and relax with that knowledge?

"Fine, I'll do my best to find the culprits. But I'll need your help," he told the woman.

"No way. If the Cacciatores find out that we've asked you to do this, they won't trust you either."

The situation sounded horribly complicated and fraught with danger from every direction. Roberto wondered if it was too late to back out and concluded that it had been too late to back out from the moment he was asked it.

"By the way," the Alessio Nonna continued, "when you find the culprits, pray for their souls. If the Cacciatores don't do it first, we'll kill them."

Chapter 4

The Alessios' Nonna was the only visitor Roberto received that morning. The sin of the tree's cutting must have made everyone else regard their own sins as negligible.

Before heading home, Roberto stopped in the church to pray and reflect on the woman's request.

However unfair her demand on his time and peace of mind, Roberto had no choice but to help and do his absolute best to get the Alessios off the hook and avoid a blood feud.

But he needed help. She had made it clear that the Alessios could not help him. Then who could he ask for help?

He needed someone who knew the town and its intimate affairs, but who could also keep the secret about the reasons for Roberto's involvement. Unfortunately, the people who had their ears on the town's grapevine were usually also its most generous feeders.

Unable to think of a solution, Roberto entrusted himself to God and headed home.

The midday sun was relentless and the shadeless streets were empty. In his black shirt and trousers, Roberto felt he was being barbequed. How much more comfortable it would be to wear the white habit of a Carthusian monk, he thought. In fact, being a monk of any kind would have been much better than being a diocesan priest: living in a convent—even better, as a hermit—would certainly stop troublesome people dumping their problems on him.

By the time he got to the door of his parents' flat, Roberto was sweaty, hungry and in a tiresome mood.

His brother's voice drifted from the dining room. His mind occupied with the Alessios' request, Roberto had completely forgotten about Corrado's arrival.

"…the Director told me, 'Well done, Corrado! The Vatican Observatory would grind to a halt without you. In fact, I doubt even the stars would move without you!'."

"I always knew you were a star!" their mum exclaimed, clapping.

Roberto walked into the dining room and found his parents and his brother having lunch. It was a family rule that meals couldn't start without everyone at the table.

"Oh, hello, Roberto. Sorry we've started without you, but Corrado was hungry after his trip," his mother apologised.

"Don't worry, Mum. Roberto doesn't mind," Corrado said.

"Your portion is in the kitchen," their mother told Roberto.

Roberto gladly left the room and Corrado's stories of his successes at the Vatican's astronomical observatory.

It was normal that his parents would be more interested in Corrado's work than in his own. Corrado's job was unique—an astronomer priest—while Roberto was only an assistant parish priest, who were ten a penny.

Roberto scraped the bottom of the pasta pot, microwaved his plate of sticky spaghetti and lingered in the kitchen for as long as he could without his family noticing and accusing him of jealousy. Then he padded back to the dining room.

"Corrado doesn't mind sharing his bedroom with you, Roberto," his mother informed him with a pleased smile.

She clearly didn't even imagine that Roberto might mind—but he did. He wouldn't have anywhere to retreat to and be alone after the stressful days of investigations ahead of him.

There was a comfortable sofa in the living room. His parents went to bed early, and if Corrado retreated to his room in good time, Roberto could have the living room to himself early in the evenings.

"I don't mind taking the sofa," he suggested, trying not to sound ungrateful.

"Don't refuse your brother's kindness," his

father reproached him. "You're old enough—and a priest too—to get over your rivalry with your brother." Then he turned back to Corrado with a smile. "Please, continue your story about the astronomy conference."

Roberto stifled a sigh.

Despite the meal having already started when Roberto joined it, it was still nowhere near ending. After a first and a second course, there was fruit and dessert. Roberto didn't remember having such a feast laid out for his arrival. He pushed the unchristian thought out of his mind, and concentrated on enjoying the food.

After lunch, Corrado announced that he needed a siesta and retreated to their bedroom, closing the door.

The sofa in the living room was taken up by their father watching a football match, and the lounger on the balcony was being grilled by the Sicilian afternoon sun.

Having nowhere to rest, Roberto decided to go out and begin his investigations into the cutting down of the *Abies*. The obvious starting point was Rosaria Pace. Roberto knew where she lived, so he set off to her flat.

Chapter 5

"Thank you for visiting a woman in disgrace!" Rosaria exclaimed when she opened the door to Roberto.

Her eyes were red-rimmed and her expression was desolate.

"I haven't opened the door to any callers today, but I know that you've come to bring comfort—not to tell me off or ask what happened."

"I haven't come to tell you off," Roberto confirmed.

However, he had come to ask her what had happened. He would have to be very tactful if he wanted to get any information without distressing her.

"Come in, Roberto, sit down," she instructed, leading him to the sitting room before disappearing into the kitchen.

Roberto hoped she wasn't making him a coffee, because he had just had one at home. But he couldn't ask her not to make one unless she offered it. So he could only wait.

The sitting room was dotted with well-dusted ornaments: vases, figurines and framed crocheted pictures on the walls. Everything was extremely tidy except for a thick fleece blanket abandoned on the sofa, crumpled. It must be the infamous blanket she had gone home to fetch last night.

Roberto guessed that, if Rosaria hadn't meant to return to the woods but had gone home to spend the rest of her nightshift in her bed, she wouldn't have taken that blanket out of her cupboard. In the heat of summer, in fact, a blanket that thick would surely not be out and in current use.

Roberto picked it up and examined it. Bits of grass and dead leaves stuck in the fabric confirmed that Rosaria had indeed returned to the woods with her blanket.

Then how could the tree cutters have taken the tree down without Rosaria noticing? Surely a tree of that size could not be cut in the time Rosaria walked home, got the blanket and walked back. Moreover, wouldn't she have noticed immediately that the tree was missing, and raised the alarm in the middle of the night? Maybe Rosaria had taken a couple of hours' nap at home before returning to the woods.

Roberto was trying to work out a way to ask his questions tactfully, when she returned with a tray laden with coffee and biscuits.

"Thank you, but I've already had a coffee at home," he told her.

She dismissed his protest with a wave of her hand and put a coffee cup in front of him together with a plate piled with biscuits.

"You mustn't be polite with me. Remember that I've known you since your mother pushed you around in a pram."

Roberto resigned himself to drinking another coffee.

"I'm an afflicted woman," she began. "Everyone blames me for the *Abies* as if I had cut it down with my own hands. But God knows that I didn't do anything wrong. All I did was go home to get a blanket, then I immediately returned to the woods. But nobody believes me," she continued, her voice breaking.

"I believe you," Roberto reassured her.

"Thank you. Everyone else thinks that I slept at home and then returned to the woods in the morning. But that's not true. I went back immediately."

"I believe you," Roberto repeated.

Having confirmed that he wasn't one of her accusers, Rosaria was now desperate to tell her story.

"The tree was still there when I went back, and there was no sign of anything amiss. The problem is"—she looked at the floor—"that I fell asleep. I don't know how it happened, because I wasn't at all comfortable on that chair in the cold night. But when I woke up, it was already light, and the tree was gone. All that was left was a stump."

"You weren't woken up by the noise of chainsaws or other machinery?" Roberto enquired.

The tree-cutters must have used heavy machinery if they didn't just cut the tree down but also dragged it away.

"Not at all. I saw and heard nothing. Nobody believes me—and I can scarcely believe it myself—but that's what happened. So I have no fault because we are allowed to fall asleep during our sit-in shift. We are just not allowed to leave the chair. That's why we always take coffee and biscuits with us, and we leave some for the people on shift after us—if the birds leave them any."

Once Roberto had learnt from Rosaria everything she knew, and had reassured her and comforted her, he set off for the woods to check out the crime scene.

Roberto found the tree stump, hastily cut and left jagged. It was surrounded by disturbed ground where the caterpillar tracks of heavy machinery were impressed on the soil. Branches had been broken off the surrounding trees. It wasn't surprising that those who had cut the last specimen of such a special fir tree hadn't cared about sparing damage to other plants.

The police had cordoned off that area so he couldn't get any closer, but what he could see was enough: a hole in the tree canopy staring back at him like a gaping wound.

Unless another specimen of *Abies nebrodensis* was found in these mountains, it was the end of this species. Scientists might be able to revive the species by germinating seeds that they had stored in their laboratories, but it would always be a repopulation. The last wild *Abies nebrodensis* had gone.

A knot formed in Roberto's throat at the thought, and he shyly glanced around to see if there were any witnesses to his emotional moment, but the person doing the sit-in was sleeping in her lounger and there was no one else there at the time of after lunch naps.

Roberto inspected the ground for clues, but it was hard to tell which footprints had been left by the lumberjacks and which had been left by the many people who had come for the inauguration of the sit-in, the previous day.

Roberto followed the caterpillar tracks up to the road, where unfortunately they disappeared. Someone had taken the trouble to brush off any debris in both directions so that it was impossible to guess which way the loggers had gone.

Sitting on the milestone, Roberto thought

about the situation. Nothing made sense. Why take all this trouble to remove the trunk from the crime scene? Just cutting the tree down would have been enough to remove the main obstacle to the building of the new road.

Unless the lumberjacks were not interested in the road at all, and they had taken the opportunity to strike when the blame would fall on someone else—the Cacciatore family.

But if the new road had nothing to do with this crime, then the possibilities were endless, and Roberto would have no idea where to begin his investigations.

As he trudged back to the town under the baking sun, Roberto heard someone call him.

"Robertino!"

Very few people still called him by his childhood nickname. One of them was his primary school teacher, Maestra Gambino.

"Maestra, hello!" Roberto greeted her with pleasure.

Maestra Gambino had been like a mother for the children of Vicina. Her job hadn't stopped at teaching the curriculum, but she had applied plasters to scraped knees, arbitrated quarrels and fed the children who needed it.

The whole town had sat at the desks of her classroom, and even those who hadn't enjoyed school still had good memories of her.

Roberto had always been a lover of books and academic learning, and during his childhood, Maestra Gambino had been his portal to this world.

"I didn't know you were back," she told him with pleasant surprise.

"I haven't been back long. I was planning to pop round and say hello but other things got in the way."

"Why don't you come over now? I was just heading home."

"Sure."

Roberto took Maestra Gambino's shopping bags from her and accompanied her home.

He remembered the two-storey house on one of the roads leading off the high street. Inside, the house hadn't changed since he used to go with his classmates for tea and cakes. The only difference was that, back then, everything had looked much bigger to him. Now he wondered how Maestra could have fitted so many children in her sitting room.

"Sit down and tell me everything you've been up to since I saw you last," she instructed him in her old teachery tone.

Roberto recounted how he had had to recover a stolen engagement ring and, subsequently, rescue Father Pietro who had been abducted by the local criminal boss.

"So you've become a bit of a detective, have you?" she asked him.

"I wouldn't say that, and I certainly haven't enjoyed any of it."

"But sometimes situations call us and we have step up and do what's needed—like I had to do with Vito."

Roberto remembered Vito very well. He had been in Maestra Gambino's class with Roberto, always coming to school with dirty, torn clothes and no snack for the mid-morning break.

In hindsight, Roberto realised that he might not have had any lunch waiting for him at home either. Maestra Gambino had always had clean clothes, food and books for him. She had taken him under her wing like an aunt.

"What's he up to?" Roberto asked.

"He works for a company in Milan. I think it imports food, but I'm not sure. He explained it to me, but I can't remember."

She poured two cups of coffee and Roberto wished he had noticed her preparing coffee earlier. It was too late to refuse now.

Then she gave him news of other people who had been in his class.

"I'm impressed that you can remember exactly who was in my class, after all these years and with all the children you've taught. I can barely remember the names of my current parishioners."

Maestra Gambino chuckled. "You've never had this gift, but you've always had plenty of others. That's why I'm not surprised that you've turned out to be a good detective. And I hope you'll apply your detective skills to the case of the tree."

"It's a difficult case," Roberto admitted.

She smiled. "I'm glad that you say that."

"Why?"

"Because it means that you're already working on it."

Roberto chuckled. Maestra Gambino was still as smart as he remembered.

"I'd welcome any help," Roberto told her.

"Of course. I will tell you anything I find out. I've heard a lot of speculations but, unfortunately, nothing worthy of notice so far. Of course, everyone thinks that the Cacciatores are behind it, but I don't think they are. They had no need to do anything so drastic."

"It's a baffling case," Roberto admitted.

"But I'm sure you'll solve it. And when you do, please, let me know who the culprits are before you hand them over to the police. I'd love a chance to give them a piece of my mind."

Roberto chuckled. A telling-off from

Maestra Gambino would be just what those people deserved.

Chapter 6

That evening, Roberto was well-caffeinated when he climbed onto the top bunk.

"Stop shaking the bed," Corrado complained from the bottom bunk.

He'd always had the bottom so that he didn't have to climb up and down the metal ladder.

"I'm not shaking anything. I'm only turning."

"Then you must have got fatter because you're causing an earthquake. Just go to sleep."

"I can't. I've had too much coffee."

"That was silly. I do worry about your diet," Corrado said.

"There's nothing wrong with my diet," Roberto snapped. It had been a long and stressful day. "If you knew all the worries I've got on my mind, you'd be kinder."

Roberto immediately regretted sharing his weakness. Corrado was bound to put him down about it.

"I'm sorry, brother. What's worrying you?" his brother asked kindly, instead.

Roberto was so taken by surprise by Corrado's reaction, and so touched by it, that despite his decision not to tell anyone, he told him everything.

"In summary, the Alessios Grandma has roped you in and now you're stuck with a task you didn't ask for or want," Corrado concluded sympathetically.

Roberto felt a little lighter. Even if his brother couldn't help him practically, at least now Roberto felt he wasn't completely alone with the problem. "You understand."

"Absolutely. Especially as I find myself in a similar situation," Corrado said.

"Really? What happened to you?" Roberto asked with sympathy.

"You've just told me about the Alessios, so now the problem is mine too. I have to help you."

Roberto leaned over the edge of the bed to check his brother's expression and understand if he was joking. Corrado looked completely serious.

"Well, if you're happy to help me…"

"I'm not happy, but I will," Corrado replied.

"Then, all the more, thank you."

"Nonsense. Now, stop wasting my time and go to sleep," Corrado said grumpily, poking Roberto through the mattress.

This was the Corrado he knew. Reassured by his brother's return to normality, Roberto finally fell asleep.

He woke up early the next morning, chilled by the sparkling mountain air. The previous evening, in fact, Corrado had insisted on leaving the window open all night, given that there were two of them in the room.

Moving as little as he could so as not to wake his brother, Roberto reached for his prayer book he had taken up to his bunk the night before.

"Please, give me Your wisdom so that I can make the right decisions and act with love today," he prayed when he had finished reciting the morning prayers from the book.

Then he took a deep breath to ready himself to start the day, and padded as quietly as he could down the ladder—only to discover that his brother wasn't in bed.

Roberto found Corrado in the kitchen, having a delicious-looking breakfast of coffee, croissant, toast with jam and a cut-up peach.

"There you are, sleepy head," he greeted Roberto. "I had wondered if I should wake you up, but then decided to give you a lie in."

"It's not even seven o'clock—that's hardly a lie-in," Roberto retorted.

He didn't like to be made to feel like a lazy sloth.

"We have a busy day ahead, and I've been waiting for you. Have your breakfast and get ready," Corrado instructed him.

Was this the way Corrado was going to help him in his investigations—taking charge and bossing him around?

Their father had just joined them in the kitchen. "What are you two doing today?" he asked them.

Roberto suddenly realised that he had never told Corrado to keep quiet about their investigations.

"Just this and that," Roberto replied quickly.

Unsatisfied, their father turned to Corrado.

"Nothing much," Corrado repeated loyally.

"Quite right—you're on holiday. Just don't get swept up in the craziness that's catching this town."

"What craziness?" Roberto asked.

"Our townsfolk seem to have lost their minds over that tree. Some are saying that the tree was killed by a poison in the water or in the soil, just because of what's happened to the birds. But how can a poison make a tree disappear? Even more ridiculously, others are convinced that the tree was pulverised by a curse. But what a about the stump with the chainsaw marks?"

Roberto stopped preparing his coffee. "What do you mean by 'what's happened to the birds'?"

"Oh, it's not even worth talking about," his father said dismissively. "Some of the women doing the sit-in have found a couple of dead birds around the stump and have got all excited about it."

Roberto put down the cafetiere as a thought suddenly struck him. Could this be the answer to how the loggers had managed to cut the tree down without Rosaria noticing?

He put the cafetiere back on the shelf. "Quick, Corrado, we must go to the woods!"

Chapter 7

Corrado had always been a faster runner than Roberto, and now he'd also had coffee and breakfast, while Roberto had had neither and was struggling to keep up. Unfortunately Corrado only stopped if Roberto did, which meant that Roberto could never bridge the gap and Corrado got to the woods first.

"Thank you for coming," the women gathered around the tree stump told Corrado. "A priest is just what we need to drive out this curse."

But as they noticed Roberto arriving too, the women got a little apprehensive.

"This must be a very powerful curse for Father Andrea to send not one but two younger priests instead of dealing with it himself," they said.

"There's no curse, but there might be sleeping powder in the refreshments you've been sharing," Roberto explained, a little breathless. "So don't touch these biscuits." He whipped a napkin open and dropped it on the tray.

"What do you mean?" the women asked incredulously.

"Sleeping powder would have killed the birds that pecked on your biscuits and would have made Rosaria Pace sleep so soundly that she didn't hear the loggers when they cut down the tree."

Roberto remembered that the person doing the sit-in yesterday afternoon had also been asleep.

"I baked those fig rolls, and I didn't put any sleeping powder in them!" the baker's wife protested, offended.

"I didn't think you did," Roberto replied calmly. "But someone else could have injected anything into them after you baked them. Would you be able to tell if someone had injected a colourless and tasteless liquid into the filling?"

Roberto glanced at the delicious-looking fig rolls that were still visible under the napkin and wished he had had breakfast before leaving the house.

"How dare they tamper with my biscuits!" The baker's wife shook her fist at her invisible foes. "Nobody eat my biscuits! Let's throw them in the bin!"

"No, don't!" Roberto said. "We must give them to the police to analyse. If they've been laced with sleeping powder, they are evidence of the crime."

Everyone agreed and someone called the police. Meanwhile, the others chased away any birds trying to peck at the delicious-looking bites.

As Roberto didn't want people to realise that he was investigating this case, he and Corrado set off back to town before the police arrived.

"How did you work out that the biscuits had been laced?" Corrado asked Roberto as they walked up a quiet road.

"When I heard that the birds had died, I remembered Rosaria telling me that the women always take refreshments to the sit-in and the birds peck at them. Sleeping powder in the biscuits explained why Rosaria hadn't woken up when the loggers cut the tree down, why the birds had died and why I found the next person on the sit-in also asleep."

"Who do you think spiked the biscuits?"

"I don't know. All I know is that it couldn't be one of the women. If any of them had wanted to cut the tree down, she would have had it done during her own shift. I think someone was watching the sit-in post from a distance. When they saw Rosaria leave the post unattended to go and get her blanket, they took advantage of it to lace the biscuits. But I have no idea who that could be."

Roberto glanced at the bougainvillea-clad fences of the wealthier homes of Vicina. The culprits could be anywhere, even in these well-to-do homes. Where would he start investigating?

"Are you worried about the Alessios?" Corrado asked Roberto.

"Of course. I don't want anyone to get hurt, even if they are criminals themselves. The *Abies* is enough."

"I meant, are you worried that the Alessios will hurt you if you don't deliver what they asked?"

"I hadn't thought about it, but I guess I should worry about that too."

"Have they threatened you in any way?"

"No."

"Let me know if they do," Corrado said in a big-brother way.

Roberto bristled. He was a grown-up man, not a little child anymore. He didn't need his big brother to fight the bullies for him. But then he decided to give his brother the benefit of the doubt: maybe he wasn't putting him down but being kind.

"Once you've discovered who's cut the tree down, what will you do?" Corrado continued.

"I'll tell the police and the most active town gossips so that the Cacciatore can find out immediately."

"Have you thought about what will happen to the tree-cutters?" Corrado asked.

"I guess they'll go to prison." A thought

suddenly occurred to Roberto. "Oh, no."

If the Cacciatore got to the tree cutters before the police, they would unleash the vendetta they were planning for the Alessios on them instead.

Roberto stopped walking and turned to face his brother, who stopped too.

"What am I going to do?" Roberto asked his brother in anguish. "If I don't find the culprits, the Cacciatores will get their revenge on the Alessios and start a blood feud. If I find the culprits, the Cacciatore—or the Alessios, whoever gets to them first—will kill them. I can't see any way in which nobody gets hurt."

"The second option should have fewer murders," Corrado said pragmatically. "But yes, neither option is ideal. Unless you find the culprits, tell Cacciatores—so that the Alessios are off the hook—then somehow help the culprits escape, for example, emigrating to another continent."

"You are suggesting that I should go to great lengths and undergo considerable danger to help the people who cut down a tree I loved and extinguished a species."

"Seventy times seven is how many times Jesus tells us to forgive others, remember?" Corrado pointed out.

Roberto turned to the woods they had just

left. The wind blowing on that side of the hill had bent the trees in a way that they looked like hands raised in supplication. It was a request for help, though, not for vengeance, Roberto thought.

"That tree meant a lot to me. I was sitting under its canopy when I first felt called to the priesthood."

"I'm sorry. I didn't know that. And there I was, thinking that it was me entering the seminary that gave you the idea."

"I'm not a copycat."

"I didn't mean that. I just thought I had been an inspiration for you."

Corrado sounded crestfallen, and Roberto felt sorry for his sharpness.

"Perhaps you were an inspiration to me, in a subliminal way," Roberto corrected himself. "Mum and Dad certainly would have hoped so."

"What do you mean?" Corrado asked.

"They've always encouraged me to follow your example. You're their perfect son."

Corrado snorted with laughter. "I think you'll find that you are their perfect son."

"You must be kidding."

"I'm not. They've always preferred you. But it doesn't matter. I've got used to it now."

"It's the other way round, Corrado."

Roberto couldn't believe this conversation. Corrado was their family's golden child.

"Then explain to me why, last Christmas, Mum and Dad travelled to Palermo to visit you and they've never come to see me in Rome," Corrado challenged him with sudden sharpness. "Who would choose to visit a ramshackle parish in a hovel of a city instead of the Vatican Observatory in the Eternal City? Mum and Dad chose Palermo because of you."

There was hurt in Corrado's voice.

"You know why they visited me last Christmas, don't you? It was not something that makes parents proud," Roberto reminded him.

Roberto had been charged in connection with an armed robbery, and had been forbidden from travelling out of Palermo, so their parents had gone to see him instead.

"But they still came to you, even if they hate travelling."

"That's why they haven't travelled to Rome. It's a lot further than Palermo."

Corrado hesitated. He clearly couldn't find a counterargument. "You haven't come to visit me either," he added, sulkily.

"But I mean to."

Corrado shot him a suspicious look. "I'll believe it when it happens."

Chapter 8

The sky was a riot of red, pink and mauve when Roberto and Corrado returned to the woods. The forensic police had been and gone, and there were only two women left.

Ashamed of their failure to protect the *Abies*, the sit-in committee had decided to double their efforts: not one but two women would be manning the sit-in post at any time.

Hearing the two women discuss who they would and would not share their shift with, Roberto was glad he wasn't organising their roster.

However, his job wasn't much easier. If his theory of the sleeping powder was correct, someone must have been watching the sit-in post from a distance, waiting for an opportunity to spike the biscuits.

But the tree canopy was dense, the tree trunks too slim to hide anyone other than a small child, and there was no substantial bushy undergrowth. He knew from his childhood that these woods were no good to play hide-and-seek.

"What are you thinking?" Corrado asked Roberto as he circled the tree stump for the third time.

"I'm not. I'm listening," Roberto replied quietly.

Sitting on their chairs, a little distance away but still within earshot, the two sit-in women were still discussing the roster.

"I can't do evenings. My husband worries about me when I go out in the evening," Franca Cascio, the accountant's wife, told the other.

"What can he possibly worry about, if he can see you from his window?" her companion replied.

She gestured towards a row of three-storey buildings on the edge of the woods—presumably her friend's home.

Roberto looked at the buildings. They had a perfect view of the woods. Even when the *Abies* was still standing, the sit-in's camp light would have been visible through the canopy. Someone could have kept a watch over the sit-in post from any of those buildings.

"I've got it!" Roberto exclaimed.

Corrado smiled. "I knew you would."

Roberto was too distracted by his thoughts to notice that his brother had paid him a compliment.

"Come, let's go!" he told Corrado.

The intercom buttons had name tags for each flat so it was easy to work out who lived on which floor and on which side of the buildings.

Roberto ruled out all the ground floor flats, as they had no view of the woods. Same for the flats looking out onto the back and those with an obstructed view.

This left only three flats. One of them was the Cascios'.

They had two doorbells, one for the home and one of Signor Cascio's accountancy office which, according to the plaque by the door, was still open. Roberto buzzed the intercom and the building's door clicked open almost immediately.

They climbed the stairs and found Signor Cascio was waiting at the door.

"I must be a very bad sinner if I've been sent not one but two priests! I hope this is not the Last Judgement because I haven't prepared my accounts for that yet," the man joked.

"Nothing as momentous as that," Roberto replied. "We've only come to ask a few questions."

"Interesting. I'm usually the one asking questions to my clients. But come in and take a seat, and we'll see what I can do to help you."

Signor Cascio led them into a surprisingly bare room except for a large desk with some chairs and a laptop.

"I had imagined your office full of filing cabinets and bookcases. Our parish office is bursting with them," Roberto couldn't help noticing.

Signor Cascio chuckled. "That's old school. Everything is online now. These days I hardly touch any paper."

Or perhaps do any work at all, Roberto thought, noticing the game app which was still running on the phone on his desk. Could this office be a front for other—illegal—activities?

"Is this the question you wanted to ask me—how to modernise the workings of the Catholic Church?"

Corrado bristled. "I work in the Vatican's astronomical observatory and I can assure you that the Catholic Church is perfectly in step with the times. We pride ourselves on state-of-the-art technology and cutting-edge research."

"I'm sure you do," Signor Cascio retorted, waving a dismissive hand. "Then to what do I owe the pleasure of your visit?" he asked in a slightly mocking tone.

"We were wondering if you could show us the view from your balconies and windows," Roberto asked politely.

No good would come from antagonising a man whose cooperation they needed.

Signor Cascio sighed. "If you're wondering if I saw the tree being cut, the answer is no. I was fast asleep. I've already told the police and proved it on my sleep-monitoring watch. I was in the deepest of sleeps."

"That could easily be faked, if you weren't the one wearing the watch, for example," Corrado put in.

Roberto squirmed. Accusing Signor Cascio when they still needed his help couldn't be a wise move.

Signor Cascio frowned. "Are you insinuating that I've lied? Why would I do that, anyway?"

"We didn't mean that at all," Roberto put in.

"Your brother did," Signor Cascio said.

"Corrado is a scientist, so he's got a habit of challenging certainties."

"Then your brother should start by challenging all the certainties around God that your church upholds with no proof."

Roberto braced himself for the argument that was sure to follow. If Roberto knew his brother, Corrado would not let Signor Cascio's barb lie, and the two men would lock horns over topics that had nothing to do with their investigation.

"Our theologians do plenty of that too," Corrado replied tersely.

"Good for them too. Well, now that I've told you that I haven't seen anything and have no information about the cutting of that tree, is there anything else you want from me? I'm a busy man."

Roberto refrained from shooting a pointed glance at the phone on the desk.

"We would be very grateful if you could show us the view from your windows anyway," Roberto said congenially.

"Why? I didn't think this investigation was anything to do with you."

"I was very fond of that tree and I'm hoping to help the investigations in whatever way I can."

"So that you can exact your own revenge? The days of the Holy Inquisition are over, my Reverend Fathers."

Corrado took a deep breath, as if about to reply.

"Perhaps it's time we left," Roberto put in quickly, standing up. "Thank you for your time."

"Any time," Signor Cascio replied insincerely.

As the accountant showed them to the door, Roberto noticed a framed certificate on the corridor's wall.

"What is this?" Roberto asked him.

"A certificate in recognition of my services to the environment. I'm the founder of Vicina's Botanical Watch Society. We monitor the local flora, keep a database of rare species and flag any concerns we have to the authorities or larger environmental watch groups. The *Abies nebrodensis* had been on our watchlist since our foundation ," Signor Cascio said. "I thought you knew."

"No. I must have already left Vicina when you started the society," Roberto said, genuinely surprised.

"I guess you had. You priests take forever studying at your seminaries. What is there so much to study, I can't fathom it. Being a priest can't be rocket science…"

Corrado cleared his throat to speak but Roberto interrupted him again.

"I'm sorry we doubted you. We've clearly been barking up the wrong tree. You must be as upset as we are about the tree's demise."

"Quite so," Signor Cascio said tersely.

Signor Cascio closed the door behind them and Roberto and Corrado were left alone on the landing.

"It can't have been him," Corrado said in a tone that suggested he had hoped for the contrary.

"As we are still inside the building, we should take the chance to check the common areas. The stairwell windows could have views over the woods," Roberto suggested.

He welcomed a short respite before confronting the residents of the other two flats.

Corrado agreed that it was a good idea. They checked every stairwell window and the access to the roof—which was locked. No freely available window had a view on the woods.

"Whoever spiked the biscuits must have kept a watch over the woods from one of the two flats we haven't seen yet," Roberto concluded as he and Corrado climbed down the stairs from the roof.

"Roberto Monti!" someone greeted him.

Chapter 9

Despite the beard and the thinning hair, Roberto immediately recognised his old classmate.

"Vito! What are you doing here?"

Seeing Vito again was a great pleasure and a welcome distraction from the crime investigations.

"That's what I should ask you," Vito replied, looking at the stairs from which Roberto and Corrado had emerged. "There's nothing up there except for the lift's service hatch and the roof."

"Corrado and I got lost," Roberto answered vaguely. He had never been a good liar, so he quickly moved on. "What a coincidence! Only yesterday Maestra Gambino and I talked about you. She told me that you work for a company that imports food, but she couldn't explain more."

"Food is just one of the many things we deal with. It's an import-export business and, actually, I own it."

"That's impressive, well done!" Roberto said from the bottom of his heart.

Vito hadn't had the best of starts in life, and he certainly hadn't had any leg-up from his family.

"Thank you," Vito replied joylessly.

Roberto thought that he might be sad that his work had taken him away from his hometown. Sometimes he felt that way too.

"Maestra Gambino told me that you live in Milan. Do you miss Vicina?"

"Yes," Vito replied absent-mindedly. "Sorry but I have to go."

"When will you go back to Milan?" Roberto asked him, hopeful of another meeting, perhaps over a coffee.

He would love to hear about Vito's successes.

"Very soon. Sorry. Bye, Roberto. Bye, Corrado."

Vito thrust a key into the door of one of the flats and disappeared inside.

"That's a bit strange," Corrrado commented.

"What?"

"He seemed very happy to see you, then suddenly he was burning to get away from you," Corrado said.

"He was in a hurry and I was holding him back," Roberto said. "You're suspicious of everything and everyone. You've even accused the founder of the Botanical Watch Society of cutting down the last *Abies*."

"I remind you that I didn't have this crucial piece of information about him," Corrado replied, piqued.

They looked for the remaining two flats with a view over the woods.

They found one on the floor below. Mail poked out from under the door.

"I don't think anybody has been here for a while," Roberto concluded.

They searched for the last remaining flat. They found it. It was Vito's.

Corrado looked at Roberto.

"Fine. You were right to be suspicious," Roberto admitted.

They had to wait for a considerable time after they knocked before Vito finally opened the door.

"Sorry I kept you waiting, I was in the shower," Vito apologised.

His hair was perfectly dry and he was still wearing the same clothes as before. Roberto couldn't help thinking that there had been no shower but only the hope that they'd go away if he kept them waiting long enough.

"It's fine."

"What can I do for you? I'm afraid it'll have to be quick. I'm very busy."

"Are you okay, Vito?"

"Of course. Why?"

"You seem a little… preoccupied."

"You never worried about my psychological

state when we were at school. What do you want from me, Roberto?"

Roberto decided that it was time to speak plainly. "We have reasons to believe that someone with access to your flat has helped the loggers cut down the *Abies*."

Vito made to shut the door but Corrado stuck his foot in the way.

"Leave me alone, Roberto! You can't prove anything!"

"Was it you, Vito? Did you help the loggers?"

Vito tried again to close the door but Roberto put his hand on the door.

"Please, don't force me to call the police before we've had a talk. You might end up in great danger," Roberto told him sincerely.

Roberto had imagined that, when he discovered who had cut the tree down, he would feel resentful and angry at them. Instead, all he could feel now was pity for his old classmate, who looked like a panicked animal backed into a corner. Roberto couldn't even begin to imagine what could have made him help the loggers.

Vito stopped trying to push the door shut and leant against the door jamb, defeated.

"I had no one to turn to. No one to ask for advice. You two have each other. I'm alone."

Roberto had never thought of Corrado as the person he would turn to in the hour of need, but hadn't Corrado been just that—the person who had stepped up to help him?

"Can we come inside?" Roberto asked.

Having this conversation within earshot of the neighbours wasn't safe for Vito. Even if his involvement didn't reach the Cacciatores' ears, Roberto was sure that there would be plenty of angry people in Vicina who might take justice into their own hands.

"Why? You two are going to tell the police anyway," Vito said defiantly.

"The police are going to be kinder than others might be. I'm just trying to protect you."

"Protect me from who?"

"The Cacciatores. I know that they're very cross about this."

"Why should they be? They're the ones who want the road to go through the woods."

"But they don't like people taking initiative in their territory without their permission. Especially in this case, where everyone assumes that they've cut the tree down to make way for the road they want. And if they deny it, they'll look weak and powerless for not protecting their territory."

Vito opened the door wide. "Come in."

Vito's flat was as messy as Vito's situation.

In the kitchen, Vito pulled out a chair from the table, dropped heavily onto it and held his head in his hands.

"I'm in so much trouble!"

Vito burst into tears and Roberto pulled out a chair next to him and draped his arm over his classmate's back.

Uneasy by the display of emotion, Corrado busied himself filling a cafetiere with ground coffee. There was nothing that couldn't be made better by coffee, for the Vicina people.

"Don't despair. God can forgive anything, even when humans don't," Roberto told his sobbing friend as he tried to comfort him.

"But humans are going to lynch me," Vito replied between tears. "And they'd only be too right. I've only got myself to blame."

Then Vito sat back and explained that his company was in financial trouble. He had heard about the proposed road that would cut through the woods and, desperate to save his company, he had an idea for a quick cash injection.

"There are crazy rich people out there who would pay anything to have a piece of furniture made with a rare or extinct wood. The *Abies* was going to be affected by the new road even if it wasn't cut down, so I hired some lumberjacks from outside Sicily, so that they had no idea what they were doing. Organising the shipment of the wood through my company was no problem, as I've shipped wood before and I could easily pass it for an ordinary fir tree." Vito sighed.

"It was going to be perfect: everyone would think that the Cacciatores had cut the tree down to stop complaints about the new road. The police would be afraid to take on the Cacciatores so they wouldn't investigate it too hard, and the Cacciatores would be grateful to have the tree out of their way," he added.

"But that's not what happened," Roberto explained. "The Cacciatores are convinced that the Alessios have cut the tree down and are mad with them for violating their territory. A species has been wiped out and the whole town is in mourning."

"Can't the tree regrow from the stump?" Vito asked.

"You mean like in coppicing? No, you can't coppice a fir tree: if you cut it down, it doesn't regrow. It just dies. Did you not know?"

Vito shook his head and hiccuped. "I'm so sorry."

"You should have paid more attention in Maestra Gambino's lessons," Roberto couldn't refrain from saying.

At the mention of their beloved teacher,

Vito sank his face in his hands and cried louder.

Chapter 10

By the time the police's forensic lab confirmed that the biscuits had been laced with sleeping powder, Vito had already confessed everything. He was taken into custody as much for his protection as for any other reason. And Roberto immediately went to Maestra Gambino's house.

This time he declined the coffee as soon as he saw her starting to prepare it.

"I'm sorry I didn't manage to tell you before the news exploded. Vito handed himself in to the police before I'd had a chance."

Vito was so worried about the Cacciatores's revenge that he had run to the police station and handed himself in, begging them to lock him up, as soon as he'd finished telling Roberto his sorry story.

"I know," Maestra Gambino said with a sad smile. "I've visited him in his cell and we've had a chat. He gave the police my name as his closest friend and contact. I told him how shocked and disappointed I am."

Roberto could imagine how ashamed Vito must have been in front of the woman who had saved him from his parents' neglect when he was a small, vulnerable child. Roberto remembered from his schooldays how upsetting the maestra's scoldings were, even though she never raised her voice nor resorted to ridicule or humiliation.

"Vito is alone in the world," Roberto reminded her under a swell of compassion. "He has no one to talk to when he's worried, to give him advice or talk him out of madcap ideas."

The maestra sighed. "I shouldn't have lost touch with him when he left Vicina. As he had turned eighteen, I assumed that he was an adult and didn't need me any more. I didn't want to hang onto him like a clingy mother, when I didn't even have a mother's rights."

"I'm sure you qualify as an honorary mum."

"I've loved him as if he were my own child," she said wistfully. "Thank you for the insight, Roberto. From now on, I'll keep watch over him. I won't let go. What a pity that it's too late."

"It's only too late for the tree and a prison sentence, but it's not too late to save Vito's life."

"What do you mean?"

"I fear that the Cacciatores or some of our fellow townsfolks will not be satisfied with any punishment inflicted by the Law."

Roberto had forgiven Vito as soon as he'd seen his friend's desperation. It had been easier than he had expected. But those who weren't

Vito's childhood friends or whose hearts were hardened by a lifetime of crime might not be as forgiving.

"I see your concern," Maestra Gambino agreed. "What can we do to protect him?"

"I'm not sure it will work, but I have an idea," Roberto said. "Let's go and talk to Vito."

***

Vito wasn't at all keen on a public apology.

"I'm terrible at speaking in public," he told Roberto, who suspected that it wasn't just that.

Seeing the faces of the people affected by his crime must be upsetting. Facing their anger, Roberto imagined, would be downright scary. But if Vito managed to do it, he would not only have a better chance of being forgiven by the town, but also by the Cacciatores.

The Cacciatores didn't care about the *Abies*, but only about their image. Vito's apology would restore that.

"It will be good practice for when you stand up in front of the court," Roberto replied to him pointedly. "If the town forgives you, the judges might be more lenient when it comes to decide your sentence. Have you any other idea of how to make amends?"

Vito hadn't, so the public apology was agreed.

A police escort would accompany him to the

woods where, by stump of the *Abies*, he would deliver his apology to the women of the sit-in and anybody who bothered to turn up.

Roberto, Corrado and Maestra Gambino spread the word around the town and, on the allotted day, a considerable crowd turned up, including the local press.

"You didn't tell me that there would be so many people," a rattled Vito complained to Roberto. "The whole town is here. All these people hate me."

"If they've bothered to come, it means that they're willing to forgive you," Roberto reassured him.

Vito's lawyer reminded him to say as little as possible, to refrain from giving any details and certainly not to mention any crime he hadn't already confessed. Vito reassured him that he had nothing left to hide.

"Just speak from your heart and let everyone feel how genuinely sorry you are," Roberto advised him.

Then Roberto gave Vito a stool to stand on, so that he could be seen by everyone.

"I feel like I'm stepping onto the gallows," Vito said.

"You're not. Stop being melodramatic," Roberto replied firmly.

Then he invited the crowd to be silent. Vito

swallowed and began.

"I want all you to know how terribly sorry I am about what I've done. I was desperate. I needed quick cash to save my company from going under, and I thought that I could just coppice the *Abies* and sell the wood, while new shoots would sprout back from the stump. I didn't realise that—oof!"

A cream cake landed on Vito's face with a squelchy splat.

"This is for our *Abies*!" someone shouted.

Another cake landed on Vito's chest. "And this is for drugging the women of Vicina!"

Rotten food followed the cakes.

"Traitor!" people were shouting.

Roberto regretted giving Vito the stool. If this wasn't the gallows, it certainly was the pillory!

"Please, let him finish!" Roberto begged the mob, but nobody was listening.

So Roberto leapt in front of Vito to shield him with his body.

"No, Roberto! Let them do it! I deserve it!" Vito protested, pushing Roberto out of the firing line.

But Roberto was clinging on. The public apology—and the stool—had been his idea. He thought he heard the crowd shout "Vito!", but maybe they were saying "Traitor!" instead.

Corrado grabbed Roberto by the dog collar and pulled him out of the firing line, while Vito's police escort picked up the sit-in chairs and used them as shields to protect Vito.

"Why did you pull me away?" Roberto protested to Corrado.

"Let him have the rotten tomatoes. He wants them."

Vito, in fact, was posing like a martyr in a painting, looking skyward as the rotten fruit rained on.

Roberto, instead, looked down at his clothes. He had shaving foam on one arm, eggs on the other, watermelon on his legs and what looked like chocolate mousse—but it might have been mud—on his chest. As he checked his shoes—miraculously clean—he saw something on the ground that made his breath hitch.

It was very small—not much more than a seedling—but it was undoubtedly a fir tree.

Had it been anywhere else, it could have been any type of fir. But so close to the stump of the *Abies*, with no other fir tree around, it could only have come from one of the *Abies*'s seeds. It was a miracle that it hadn't been trampled by people or machinery.

"The *Abies nebrodensis* isn't extinct!" Roberto cried out.

The pelting stopped and silence fell. Roberto pointed to the seedling and asked everyone to stand back.

"This can only have come from a seed of our *Abies*. Are there any botanists here? Professionals or amateurs, please come forward!"

Signor Cascio and the members of Vicina's Botanical Watch Society put down their shaving-foam cakes and stepped out of the crowd.

After careful examination, they unanimously confirmed that the seedling was an *Abies nebrodensis*.

"Now that it's no longer shaded by its parent tree, it will have enough space and light to grow quickly, so long as it's not trampled by people or animals," Signor Cascio declared.

Everyone cheered, Vito burst into tears of relief and hugged Roberto, transferring more shaving foam and rotten tomatoes onto him.

"I will guard the new tree with my life!" Vito pledged from his soapbox.

"Excellent idea!" his lawyer told him, rubbing his hands. "We'll ask the court to give you community service as tree guardian in place of a prison sentence."

When Roberto and Corrado got home that evening, their mum looked at Roberto and shook her head.

"Why do you always manage to get a lot dirtier than your brother?" she asked. "Stay here and don't move. I'll run a bath and call you when it's ready."

Corrado sniggered but Roberto didn't mind. It wasn't so bad being treated like a naughty child if that meant having a bath run for him. Roberto could finally see how Corrado might be just a little jealous.

Chapter 11

Roberto surprised himself with his sadness about Corrado leaving. His brother had come to the end of his holiday and it was time for him to return to Rome.

"You must come and see me at the Observatory—that's the place where I really make a difference," he told his family at the train station, where they were waving him off onto the train.

Their parents shook their heads. "You know that we don't travel."

"But you've been to Palermo to visit Roberto."

"Rome is a lot further."

"But it's also a lot more interesting," Corrado retorted, but their parents continued to shake their heads.

"But you will come, won't you?" Corrado asked Roberto.

It sounded more like a plea than a question and Roberto was torn. He had no desire to see those parts of the Catholic Church he disliked most—the wealth, the pomp and the vanity. But he felt he couldn't refuse without Corrado feeling unloved by his own family. Moreover, during his holiday Corrado had helped him in his investigation, watched his back and stood by his side—protective, generous, loving.

There was no way Roberto could refuse.

"Yes. I will."

Corrado smiled and clapped him on the shoulder. "I knew you wouldn't let me down. When?"

"I don't know yet. I can't ask for more leave from the parish at the moment."

Roberto in fact had already asked Father Pietro for a couple of days' extension to his home leave so that he could tie up loose ends in Vicina. He was especially worried about Vito's situation with the Cacciatores.

As soon as Corrado was gone, Roberto paid a visit to Maestra Gambino.

"I was hoping to see you," she told him as she prepared a coffee without asking if he wanted it. Roberto resigned himself to it.

She told him that the *Abies*'s logs had been returned to Vicina, where they would be turned into a protective cage for the seedling and a bench for people admire it.

As well as Vito, the buyer of the *Abies* was being prosecuted, the money from the sale had been confiscated, and Vito's company had been declared bankrupt.

The shock of losing the species had shaken everyone into protecting it better when given a second chance, and all plans for the road to cut through the woods had been scrapped.

"What the big tree couldn't achieve, the seedling has," Maestra Gambino commented.

"Where is the road going through instead?" Roberto asked.

"It will go between the Cacciatores' and the Alessios' territories, creating a physical border between the clans. Hopefully, this will reduce friction between them."

"What about Vito? Have the clans forgiven him?"

"The Alessios have, but the Cacciatores have sent him threats. I don't know what to do." Maestra sighed. "We certainly can't ask the police to escort Vito to the Cacciatores' boss so that he can apologise directly."

"No, Vito can't go. But you can," Roberto said.

"Me?"

"You've taught everybody in Vicina. Haven't you had at least some of Cacciatores in your classroom too?"

"Yes, I have."

"Then you could pay a visit to an ex-pupil's mum, couldn't you?"

"I guess I could." Maestra drained her coffee. "But you'll have to come with me."

They set off immediately.

The mother of Maestra Gambino's worst-ever pupil still lived in the same house on the outskirts of the town. Unlike her son's abode, which was protected by a high wall with barbed wire, CCTVs and guard dogs, Nonna Cacciatore still lived in a cottage without fences, the end of her garden marked only by the edge of her tomato patch.

She was a wiry woman with suspicious eyes, and she was waiting for them at her door.

"I knew you would come, sooner or later," she told them by way of a greeting.

It wasn't clear, at least to Roberto, if she was pleased to see them or the contrary.

She went inside without a word, and the others followed her all the way into the kitchen, where she loaded ground coffee into her moka pot and set out three cups.

Roberto wondered how much caffeine it took to kill a man of his size.

Then she sat down at the kitchen table with them and spoke.

"Ah, Maestra Gambino, if only my son was still in trouble with you rather than with the law!" she said wistfully.

The Maestra's ex pupil was the current head of the clan, after his father had been murdered.

"I wish that too," Maestra Gambino said sadly.

"When they're little, we can punish them and try to keep them on the straight path. But when they grow up, there's very little we can do."

"But we can still do something. I'm sure your son still listens to you."

"Not as much as I would like him to. He doesn't realise that I still love him like when he was my little boy."

"I know what you mean. Even if I haven't got my own children, as you know I've taken Vito under my wing since he was a little boy. This is why I've come to ask you to put in a good word for him."

Nonna Cacciatore frowned. "Vito has committed a serious crime on our patch. My son is very upset with him and would have had him shot when he gave his apology, if it wasn't for him"—she shot a bad look at Roberto—"who got in the way."

Roberto ricocheted back. He had no idea he was shielding his friend from real metal bullets rather than just rotten tomatoes. Would he have stood in the way so readily if he had known?

"There are better ways to solve problems than bullets," Roberto said.

"Bullets are our way." She sighed. "This is why my husband is no longer with us." She looked earnestly at Roberto. "I dread to imagine where he might be now."

"God is merciful towards those who repent with a sincere heart."

"But Jesus said, 'Blessed are the merciful, for they will be shown mercy'. My husband was never merciful. I can't expect God to show him mercy."

"God's mercy is beyond imagination," Roberto said.

"I wish my husband had thought about it when he was still on this earth."

"Your son is still in time to avoid repeating his father's mistakes—by showing mercy to Vito, for example," Roberto said. "You could suggest it to him."

The woman narrowed her eyes like someone who has spotted a deal. "If I do that, will you pray for my husband? Your prayers must be worth more than mine."

"I'm not sure my prayers are worth more than anyone else's but, yes, deal done."

Chapter 12

The sun wasn't yet burning when Roberto walked with his parents to the coach stop.

It was early in the day, but by no means early to return to Palermo. Roberto had exceeded his home leave by three days and he was sure that Father Pietro needed him. Also, Roberto missed his parish.

His home leave had been a change but certainly not a rest. Now he looked forward to some quiet time back in his parish, doing the things he knew how to do—celebrating the sacraments, preparing his homilies, visiting the sick and housebound.

Nonna Maria was sweeping the pavement outside her home as they approached.

Roberto greeted her and she frowned.

"Back to Palermo already?" she asked his parents, as if they were the ones sending him away.

"I'm afraid so," Roberto replied.

"Every child must flee the nest, eventually," his mother said.

Roberto felt it would be petty to point out that he had fled the nest years ago.

"Well, we can't be greedy," Nonna Maria said with a sympathetic smile. "They must need you in Palermo, too—such a clever boy."

Roberto sighed inwardly. If, one day, he

became a bishop or a cardinal—he hoped not— he would always remain a boy for his townsfolks.

Nonna Maria took his hands in hers and squeezed them. "Thank you for all you've done for our *Abies*."

Before Roberto could reply, his mum replied for him.

"No need to thank him. It was mostly Corrado's doing, of course. He's the sharp one in the family," she said.

Nonna Maria gave Roberto a sympathetic smile and let go of him. Roberto found a boiled sweet in his hands. Nonna Maria winked.

They met a few more townsfolks on the way, and they all were told the same thing by Roberto's mum: Corrado had been the one to solve the mystery of the *Abies*, and Roberto had only helped him.

When they got to the coach stop, the breeze rising from the sea up the flank of the mountain had picked up. It smelled of sea and pine trees, and it had always marked the end of summer. As a child and a teenager, Roberto had always welcomed it with a quiet excitement, looking forward to the beginning of a new academic year.

"There's no need for you to wait. The coach will be here any moment," he told his parents.

"We want to stay and wave you off. When will you come again?" his mother asked, with a hint of sadness.

"I don't know," Roberto replied candidly.

The coach turned into the road.

"Oh no, it's already here," his mother said in a maudlin tone, much to Roberto's surprise.

She took his face in her hands and looked at him tragically, as if to impress his features in her memory for the last time ever. "Come back as soon as you can. I can't live without my favourite son for too long."

The door of the coach hissed open so there was no time to elaborate on the explosive revelation.

Roberto hugged his parents and jumped onto the coach. As he waved back at them from the window—his mother dabbing her eyes with a tissue—Roberto looked forward to some peace and quiet for his heart, back in the bustling, messy, noisy city.

The End

PS. The *Abies nebrodensis* is a critically endangered species endemic to the Madonie Mountains, in Sicily, which were once called 'Nebrodes'. Nowadays the term 'Nebrodi' refers to the adjacent mountain range, further east.

Considered extinct since 1900, the Sicilian fir was rediscovered in 1957 in one valley between Mt. Scalone, Mt. Pene and Mt. Cavallo, where there are currently 25 fertile trees, all clinging to a scree, where they have little competition from more vigorous species. Efforts to propagate seeds and increase the population are being carried out by the University of Palermo and other bodies in the Madonie Mountains, in private gardens in the province of Palermo, and in botanical gardens and arboreta all over the world.

2. THE STOLEN STATUE

Chapter 1

There's no place like home, Roberto thought as he rattled his suitcase over the cobblestones of Palermo's historic centre.

The ancient churches, scattered like jewels in unexpected corners, the laundry lines stretched between balconies across narrow alleyways, the ailanthus trees growing out of crumbling mortar—all this was now more familiar to him than the mountain town where he was born and had grown up.

He turned the corner and his parish church—the place he now called home—came into view.

Roberto loved every bit of it—the baroque façade which had witnessed Palermo's heyday, when this part of the city was home to the well-heeled and highly born; the church's bell towers, still holding a full complement of cheerful bells; the columns with their ornate capitals; the niches with the statues of the saints looking down on the square like benevolent parents; the stone steps where children played games and teenagers sunned themselves. Roberto had missed all of this when he was on "home" leave at his parents' house.

Propelled by excitement, he climbed the steps to the presbytery as quickly as his trailing suitcase allowed him.

The flat's door was unlocked, guarded only by Father Pietro's empty sandals.

Roberto felt a pang of guilt as he remembered that he was in debt to his boss.

Tied up with a crime investigation in his hometown, Roberto had had to ask Father Pietro for an extension to his home leave. The parish priest had granted it readily, but not because he didn't need him, Roberto knew, but because Father Pietro's generosity was of biblical proportions.

Roberto's delayed return must have caused his boss considerable inconvenience, especially as the parish was currently running several summer activities to keep the neighbourhood children out of trouble during the school holidays.

So when he stepped into the flat, Roberto was utterly ready to grovel.

As he padded down the corridor, Roberto heard the news on TV. This was unusual, as Father Pietro didn't normally watch TV until the evening news.

Roberto found him sitting on the sofa.

"Hello, I'm back," Roberto greeted his boss sheepishly.

Father Pietro jolted with surprise. "Oh, hello. I didn't hear you come in," he replied.

He sounded just as sheepish as Roberto, and nowhere near as happy to see him as Roberto had expected.

Then Roberto noticed the leg raised on a chair, encased in a plaster cast.

"Goodness! What happened to you?"

"Nothing much. A stupid little fall."

"How did you do it?"

"Being an idiot."

"What did you break?"

"Just a silly little bone."

Roberto despaired that he would ever find out anything more than variations of the word "stupid". Then Agostino, the sacristan, emerged from the kitchen.

"Hello, Roberto! It's great to have you back!" He greeted Roberto with a hug. "Don't listen to Father Pietro. There was nothing little about that fall," Agostino clarified. "He fell off the tall ladder when he was trying to open one of the windows above the altar."

Those windows were several metres high up on the wall.

"I would have helped him," Agostino continued, "I could have at least held the ladder steady for him, but I was in the sacristy and I didn't know what he was doing. It's a miracle he got away with just a broken leg."

"I'm very sorry," Father Pietro said, looking chastened.

"You have no reason to be sorry. If there's anyone to blame, that's me," Roberto said. "If I had been here, I could have gone up the ladder in your place."

"And now I'm useless," Father Pietro continued. "Poor Agostino has had to do everything for me. I can't get dressed on my own, let alone cook or climb the steps to the altar to celebrate Mass. The only thing I can do is sit in the confessional. But the people who come for confession are more interested in asking how I broke my leg than in telling me their sins."

"That's because everyone loves you," Agostino said, patting Father Pietro's arm affectionately.

Roberto felt a swell of gratitude for

Agostino who, despite his work and family commitment, still volunteered his time to look after the parish and, now, Father Pietro too.

"I'm back now and I can help," Roberto said.

"I'm very glad because…" Father Pietro hesitated, "I have a favour to ask you."

"Sure. I'll do anything," Roberto replied with eagerness caused by guilt.

"Even taking our youth group to Lourdes?" Father Pietro asked sheepishly, studying Roberto's reaction.

Roberto instantly regretted making such a broad and unconditional offer.

Had Father Pietro asked him to officiate one hundred funerals, or to man the parish office every day, or to preside over a thousand parish meetings, Roberto wouldn't have minded so much. But a trip with teenagers was very far from his comfort zone. Besides, he had only just come back from a holiday which had been anything but restful, and he longed for some quiet time at home.

"I was supposed to take them myself, but I can't in this state. Unless someone else takes my place, the entire trip will have to be cancelled, the kids will be disappointed, and we'll lose all the money we've already paid," Father Pietro pleaded. "Besides, spending time with our kids will be a good preparation for when you start your teaching post."

That reminder of his upcoming teaching post only added to Roberto's mounting stress.

No, a trip with the teens was the last thing he wanted. Surely the best preparation for his upcoming teaching job would be rest and study.

"Can Signora Grasso go instead?" he asked.

Roberto had helped her run the younger children's summer camp and had had first-hand experience of how capable she was around young people.

"I'm afraid not. She's looking after her husband. Her daughter, Lia, will be going instead. But we still need one more adult to make up the numbers and to be the group leader. I'm sorry to ask you, Roberto. If I could think of anyone else, I wouldn't have asked you."

Roberto wondered if that would have been out of kindness or fear of his ineptitude.

"How many kids are going?"

"Thirty plus two."

"Who are the 'plus two'?"

"Tano and Enza. I've made them assistant leaders given that they're nineteen so they count as adults."

Roberto remembered having to coax a

weeping Tano out from under his bed only a couple of weeks earlier. He had his doubts about Tano's adulthood.

"Isn't Tano working at Signora Albi's?" Roberto asked.

Roberto had got Tano that job with a lot of effort—twice over. He dreaded to discover that Tano had lost it again.

"He's asked for a week off so that he could join the trip and, after a lot of begging, he's been granted it. He's very keen to go."

Roberto felt for his young friend. He could imagine how much it must have cost him to plead his case with the formidable Signora Albi. Tano hadn't had many chances in life, and he wasn't likely to get more.

This would be his first trip outside Palermo and perhaps the only chance he would ever get to travel outside Italy. Roberto couldn't deny it to him.

"Fine. I'll go," he said.

Then he dragged his suitcase—which he would not need to unpack—to his room, sat on his bed and felt like crying.

Chapter 2

That night, Roberto prayed fervently to be granted the strength, wisdom and patience he would need on this trip, because he was sure they would be sorely tested.

What he didn't know was that the testing would start before the trip.

As soon as she found out that he was replacing Father Pietro, the group's co-leader, Lia, went to see Roberto.

While he knew her mum well, Roberto had never exchanged more than a few words with Lia.

"One of the conditions for me coming on this trip was that I would only look after the girls. It's non-negotiable, and Father Pietro agreed," she informed him curtly.

As there were only a handful of girls—including Enza, the assistant leader—this was a very unequal division of labour, which testified to Father Pietro's bountiful generosity.

As he was taking Father Pietro's place on this trip, Roberto felt he had to honour these terms.

Another unpleasant surprise came when Tano discovered that Enza was on the trip too.

"I'm not going if she's going," the young man announced sulkily.

Roberto's attempts to find out the reasons

were fruitless. But as Tano was one of the assistant group leaders, it was paramount that he came on the trip. That was even before counting the fact that Roberto had agreed to go mostly for the young man's sake.

Roberto only managed to persuade him by promising he would sit next to him on the coach so that there would be no chance of Enza doing so.

This was no small sacrifice for Roberto. He suffered from travel sickness and had hoped to sit by himself on the 24-hour coach trip from Palermo to the French town in the Pyrenees, so that he could doze, pray or just be sick in peace.

When the day of the departure finally arrived, the excited kids turned up well before the appointed time and before Roberto was ready to welcome them.

At the allotted time, the coach arrived with the two coach drivers, Giordano and Elio, who would be accompanying them all through the pilgrimage. The two men—also parishioners— had volunteered to drive them to Lourdes and back in exchange for board and lodgings, as they were keen to visit Lourdes too.

Lia, however, was nowhere to be seen.

The instructions for the travel sickness pills recommended taking them half an hour before departure, and Roberto had duly done so.

But by the time Lia turned up and they were able to leave, the effect of the travel sickness pills was already wearing off on Roberto.

While Tano dropped off to sleep at the first turn of the coach's wheels, Roberto was wide awake and ready to feel every bend of the road in his stomach.

Running along the northern coast of Sicily, this panoramic route offered breath-taking views of the Tyrrhenian sea.

The straight of Messina—which separated Sicily from mainland Italy—still lacked a bridge. Earlier that month, a contract had been signed to start building one, but the project had been in the pipeline all through Roberto's life, so he wasn't holding his breath about it.

Anyway, getting off the coach and onto the ferry for the half-hour crossing gave Roberto a few precious minutes of respite from travel, until the boat set off and Roberto's motion sickness was back with a vengeance.

Then they returned into their glass-box coach and motored up the Italian boot all the way to the far west corner of the Alps and into France.

Roberto wished he could sleep but, despite a second dose of travel-sickness tablets, he couldn't.

Tano, instead, slept all the way through. Every now and then Roberto roused him to make sure that he was okay. The boy was perfectly fine.

It was Roberto who wasn't fine at all. When the coach entered the French town in the Pyrenees, Roberto was exhausted. To save the cost of a night's hostel, Father Pietro had timed the coach journey to arrive in Lourdes in the morning. Roberto now had a whole day ahead of him before his head could touch a—stationary—pillow.

A tranquil river separated the town from the sanctuary complex. The coach crossed the bridge and stopped in front of the wide, open gates.

As Roberto stepped out of the coach and saw the sanctuary grounds stretch before him in all their white stone beauty, his spirits lifted.

A long, wide avenue led the eye to the magnificent complex of three basilicas on three levels. On the upper level stood the oldest basilica, a beautiful gothic building with a tall spire flanked by two smaller ones which belonged to the middle-level basilica.

This second basilica was built in a Byzantine style, encased by ample, curved staircases and bridges, like welcoming arms. A gilded crown and cross—gifted by the people of Ireland—

sat on top of this basilica's oriental-inspired dome, shining in the sun.

Below everything, and invisible from the outside, was the newest and biggest of the three basilicas. Roberto had read that it looked like an upturned ship and that, stretching under the avenue all the way, it could host as many as twenty-five thousand people.

But the main attraction wasn't any of these grand basilicas. Instead, it was a small cave, just round the corner, set in the rocky hillock on which the basilicas were built. It was in that humble cave that, almost two hundred years earlier, a peasant girl called Bernadette had met the Mother of Jesus and had talked to her like one flesh-and-blood person to another.

Now a statue of Mary had been placed on the spot where the Blessed Mary had stood, and pilgrims queued to get close to it, touch the rock and say a prayer.

The group said goodbye to the coach driver, who went away to park, and Roberto led the party to join the long queue for the grotto.

Tired from their long trip, the teens were growing restless and were chattering, pushing and irritating each other. Lia had gone off on her own and was nowhere to be seen. Before a weary Roberto had to intervene to restore order, Enza stepped in. With a few authoritative words, she got the others to quieten down, without being unkind or bossy.

Roberto didn't know her well, but she seemed to be a kind and capable girl. Why did Tano dislike her so much?

"Look at those roses!" Enza exclaimed, to no-one in particular. "Aren't they beautiful?"

A wild rose bush grew out of a crevice in the rock—a reminder that, despite the candles, the cordons and the chairs, this was still a natural grotto.

When it was their turn to enter the cave, Roberto felt a swell of emotion. He stroked the rock made smooth by millions of pilgrims' hands over the centuries. Admiring the simplicity of that cave, he imagined the simplicity of the peasant girl who had been chosen for the job of giving this world a message from the other side.

After the grotto, they went to the taps that dispensed water from the spring Bernadette had dug out under the instruction of Mother Mary.

Before they started drinking and washing prayerfully in the spring, Roberto approached Tano.

"I don't know what Enza has done to you, but it would be a good idea to ask Mother Mary for the gift of forgiveness. Holding a grudge won't do your soul any good."

Tano shook his head. "It's complicated, Father. I can't explain it."

Then they crossed the river and lit candles as they prayed for loved ones or their own personal supplications.

Lia, who had been absent and uninterested in the trip until now, had collected gallons of spring water to take home and was now lighting candles profusely.

"She's praying for her sick dad," Tano told Roberto.

Now it all made sense. Lia hadn't come on the trip because she enjoyed being with young people or looking after them. She had come just for her dad.

Chapter 3

After a reinvigorating night's sleep, Roberto woke up feeling like new. The children must have been tired too, because there had been no trouble about going to sleep.

The youth hostel was within walking distance from the sanctuary grounds and, after a hearty breakfast of croissants, toast and Pyrenees' ham and cheeses, they set off on foot.

They were still some way off when some blue flashing lights up at the complex caught Roberto's attention. He couldn't tell if it was ambulance or police, so he reminded everyone in the group to keep a watchful eye over their possessions, just in case the problem was pickpocketing.

But when they got there, they found that the gendarmes had cordoned off the grotto, and the statue of Mother Mary was missing from its niche.

"They've stolen Mother Mary!" other pilgrims told them.

Shock and outrage rippled through their party. Some worried that, if these thieves had managed to steal Our Lady, they would surely be able to steal people's phones.

"It's only a statue. Nobody can kidnap Mother Mary," Roberto reminded the children.

He felt cross with the people who had done this—For money? For attention? To cause a stir?—and had upset the pilgrims. He resolved that he wouldn't let them upset his group.

"Come on, let's go on our way," Roberto encouraged them. "We have a lot to look forward to today."

After climbing the hill with the life-size stations of the cross, they would walk back down through the woods and take part in the Italian mass in one of the chapels. Then they'd fill their bottles with the spring's water to take home to family and friends.

"There's no point," Lia replied, shaking her head. "This whole trip is pointless now."

"Why? What the thieves have taken is only a statue," Roberto replied.

"Yes, but Our Lady will be upset and won't grant any miracles now. She might even punish us!"

"I doubt she's the vindictive kind," Roberto replied jokingly.

But Lia didn't smile and Roberto realised that she had been deeply upset by the theft.

"I'm sure Mother Mary has already forgiven the thieves—mothers are used to forgiving—and she certainly won't blame anyone else," Roberto said, more compassionately.

"But she will, and she won't cure my father!

This trip has been useless!" Lia cried and burst into tears.

A swell of panic washed over Roberto. In the seminary he had learnt to write essays on the theological meaning of human suffering, but he had no idea how to deal with someone crying in front of him. So he just stood there, helpless as a stolen statue.

Thankfully, Enza came to the rescue.

"Don't cry, Lia," she said, enveloping the other woman in a hug. "We'll all pray for your dad and will make so much noise that heaven will hear us!"

"Yes!" the others chorused, happy to be able to do something.

"And I'm sure the police will find the thieves and recover the statue very soon," Enza continued, rubbing Lia's back comfortingly. "In fact, look, they're just coming this way."

Everyone turned to look at the two gendarmes heading towards them with handcuffs open and ready. To everyone's shock, they stopped in front of Tano and clicked the handcuffs onto his wrists.

"You're under arrest," they told him in French, followed by other things Roberto couldn't understand.

Gasps rippled through the group. Tano shot Roberto a panicked look.

"There must be a misunderstanding. This young man is part of our group," Roberto told the gendarmes in French.

"This young man was climbing the cave near the statue last night. We have CCTV footage of him."

"He couldn't be. He was asleep in our hostel with everyone else," Roberto protested, and turned to Tano.

The young man's guilty look told Roberto that the gendarmes were right.

Chapter 4

The gendarmes searched the hostel but didn't find the statue there. However, they did find it in the luggage compartment of the coach.

Even if all the clues pointed to Tano, Roberto couldn't believe that Tano was responsible for such a cruel and idiotic prank.

Yes, the young man could have easily slipped out of the hostel while everyone, tired from the journey, was fast asleep. But why would he steal a statue that meant so much to so many people?

After a lot of pleading, Roberto was allowed to visit Tano in his custody cell.

The boy was sitting in a corner with his face buried in his hands. When he heard the door's lock clunk open he looked up. At the sight of Roberto, he hid his face again.

Roberto wasn't in the mood for hide and seek.

"At least have the courage to look at me," he told the young man.

Tano looked up—eyes red with tears. "I'm sorry."

"I think we'll both agree that you've got some explaining to do," Roberto said.

"I did it for Enza," Tano replied. He tipped his head back and let out a deep sigh that sounded more love-sick than guilt-stricken.

"So you admit that you did it," Roberto said, hoping to be contradicted.

"Yes, I do."

Roberto felt utterly betrayed. Roberto had always believed in Tano's inner goodness. Roberto had fought to get him a job as a housekeeper, putting his own reputation on the line. And finally, he had agreed to come on this trip to give Tano the chance of a trip of lifetime. And now Tano had done this to him.

"Did Enza ask you to do it?" Roberto asked, feeling a prick of jealousy.

"No. I just heard her say that she liked the roses."

"What roses?"

"The ones that grow on the rocks of the cave. While we were queueing to get into the cave, she said that she liked them."

Roberto remembered that comment but it still made no sense. "What have the roses got to do with stealing the statue?"

"I stole no statue," Tano replied with shock. "All I stole was one rose, that's why I climbed on the rocks. I never touched Mother Mary— not even when I was losing my footing. It wouldn't have been proper to balance myself on her."

"So you didn't steal the statue?" Roberto

repeated.

"Never! I swear!" Tano crossed himself to emphasise the solemnity of his oath.

"Did you tell the gendarmes?"

"How? I don't speak French. Why, do they think I took Our Lady? I thought they'd arrested me over the rose."

"So you didn't put the statue in the luggage compartment of our coach?"

"No," Tano said with contempt. "If I had stolen Mother Mary, I would have made her travel on a proper seat!"

Roberto felt a swell of relief. Even if Tano had broken the group's rules by sneaking out of the hostel at night, he hadn't committed a more serious crime.

It still didn't make sense why he would gone through all that trouble to pick a rose for a girl he detested, but that was a question for later— if it was any of Roberto's business anyway. Now he must tell the gendarmes what had happened.

A translator was arranged and Tano was interrogated.

Roberto learnt that the CCTV had been smashed half-way through Tano's climb so there was no proof whether he had taken the statue or just the rose. However, for the time being, Tano was the only suspect and he was remaining in custody. There was no guarantee that he would be able to travel back with the rest of the group, in three days' time. Unless, of course, the real culprit was found.

The incomplete CCTV footage, together with the fact that there were no witnesses and no fingerprints, didn't leave much to go by. Roberto had a feeling that, having found a suspect to offer the jury for trial, the gendarmes were not burning to find other leads. If Roberto wanted Tano to come home with them, he would have to find the culprit himself—and very quickly.

So Roberto was in low spirits when he stepped out of the police station and was confronted with a mob of journalists.

As soon as they saw him, they rushed to thrust their microphones and their questions at him.

"Have you taken the suspect's confession, Father?" they asked him in French.

Roberto was taken by surprise, but he immediately realised that, if they were addressing him in French, they probably didn't know that Tano was Italian. Perhaps they didn't know anything more than the fact that the gendarmes had arrested a suspect.

But if Roberto opened his mouth to say anything—even just "no comment"—they would know from his accent that he wasn't French. It wouldn't help the relations between the two countries if the thief of the beloved statue was found to be Italian.

Without a word, Roberto pushed through the journalists and walked in the opposite direction to the hostel until he was sure that none of the journalists were following him.

Chapter 5

When he finally made it back to the hostel, Roberto found Enza waiting for him.

"How is Tano?" she asked, wringing her hands in worry.

"As good as can be under the circumstances," Roberto replied.

"I hope they're feeding him all right."

Roberto had seen a tray with a delicious-looking baguette being carried towards Tano's cell as he was leaving. Roberto, who hadn't had anything since breakfast, had been quite envious. "I believe food won't be a problem."

Enza looked relieved. "Can I have a word with you?"

"Yes, I think that would be a very good idea."

The hostel's common room was empty. Roberto and Enza sat at a table where a jigsaw puzzle of cute kittens was in progress.

"It's all my fault," Enza said, looking down as if talking to the kittens. "Tano climbed the cave to get a rose for me. Did he tell you?"

"Yes, he did."

"Does anyone else know about it?"

"Only the gendarmes."

"Please, don't let anyone else find out, or Tano will be in even more trouble."

Roberto couldn't imagine Tano being in any

more trouble than he already was.

"Can you explain?" he asked.

"My dad has found out about us and he has warned Tano to keep away from me or he'll kill him. But I love Tano and he loves me." She sighed and looked out of the window, as if Tano might pop up there in one of his climbing exploits.

This explained why Tano took great pains not to be seen anywhere near Enza. And why he stole roses for her at night, when anyone who could report back to Palermo was asleep, Roberto thought.

"What will happen to Tano now?" Enza asked with worry.

"He'll have to stay here until the trial and we'll have to go home without him, unless the real culprit is found before that."

"Then you and I, Father, will find the statue's thief," Enza said resolutely.

"I think Lia will need your help more than me," Roberto replied.

Lia wasn't going to be happy to be left to look after the entire group while Roberto investigated the crime.

Enza smiled at him with tenderness, as if Roberto had said something sweet but naive. "With all respect, I think you'll need me more, Father."

***

As the statue had been found in the luggage hold of their coach, Roberto decided to start the investigations from there.

"There's no sign of breakage," he said, inspecting the lock. "Whoever put the statue here must have had keys."

"Let's talk to the drivers," Enza suggested.

They found Giordano and Elio in the hostel's cafeteria and asked them who had access to the keys of the coach.

"Just the two of us," Elio told them.

"But there's been an incident…" Giordano said. "When I woke up this morning, the keys were not where I had left them—in my shoe under my bed. I searched my trousers' pockets, my suitcase, my jacket, but I couldn't find them. I was worried, of course, but I knew that Elio had another set so I decided to have my breakfast first and look for them again later. So I went downstairs and had breakfast. When I was on the stairs, going back to my room, I saw Tano run out of it—I had left it unlocked. Surprise, surprise, the keys were back in my shoe, exactly where I had left them last night. But they weren't there when I woke up."

"Could they have been there all along but you hadn't seen them?" Enza ventured.

He shot her a disapproving glance. "My

eyesight is perfect. If it weren't, I wouldn't be allowed to drive coaches. My only mistake was leaving my room unlocked last night. But how could I imagine that that criminal boy would waltz in and steal the keys right from under the bed where I was sleeping?"

"Are you sure that the person you saw leaving your room was Tano?" Roberto asked.

"A hundred per cent sure. I've known all these kids since they were babies." Giordano sighed. "That's why it makes me very sad to see one of them go astray. I wasn't going to say anything because I didn't want to make trouble for him, but given what's happened…"

"What a rascal!" Elio exclaimed, outraged. "He stole the keys to hide his loot in our coach so that we would take it home for him—or be blamed for the theft if it was discovered before!"

It made perfect sense, Roberto thought. And yet, Tano had told him that he hadn't taken the statue and he had sounded genuine. Fear might have pushed him to lie, but Tano lacked the cunning necessary to be a convincing liar.

Roberto and Enza left the drivers to their lunch—Roberto still hungry—and hurried to the gendarmerie.

This time, the gendarmes made no trouble

about Tano receiving visitors. The young man beamed as soon as he saw Enza, and the two ran into each other's arms with fervour.

But as soon as Tano heard about Giordano's accusations, he flew into a rage.

"It's all lies—big, fat lies! You don't believe them, right?"

"Of course not!" Enza replied.

Roberto didn't reply. A lot of evidence pointed in Tano's direction now, and Roberto felt he needed more than an outraged denial to be reassured.

Roberto's silence caused Tano's eyebrows to float in shock, then outrage.

"How cheeky of you to come and see me just to accuse me! I'm not going to listen to your rubbish," Tano burst out, and made to leave.

But as he reached the armoured door, he remembered that he couldn't leave. So he turned back to Roberto.

"Go away! You're not welcome here anymore," he instructed with the authority of the host.

"You can't treat Father Roberto like this, Tano. He's only trying to help you," Enza protested, stepping in the way of the door, as if either of them could leave without the guard opening the door from the outside.

Tano harrumphed and folded his arms, refusing to apologise.

"You're being a proud ass," Enza told him.

"It's okay, Enza. Nobody is offended."

"I am," Tano said.

"You shouldn't be," Enza replied.

"We had better leave now," Roberto told Enza, judging that it was going to be impossible to get Tano to give them any useful information in his current mood.

The two lovers parted without a hug.

As they were being let out of the cell by the guard, Roberto let Enza go through the door first and hung back for a moment.

"Are you sure you don't know anything about who took the coach keys?" he whispered to Tano when Enza was out of earshot.

"I've told you all: I only stole the rose!" he shouted, and kept shouting it as Roberto and Enza walked down the corridor under the gazes of the gendarmes.

"I'm sorry that didn't go very well," Roberto apologised to Enza when they were finally outside.

They could still faintly hear Tano bellowing his innocence.

"I know you are trying to help Tano, but how can you do it if you don't believe that he's innocent?" she asked him.

"I just need him to give me some evidence, some reasons to believe him over Giordano."

Giordano was an upstanding member of the parish who had generously volunteered his time to make this trip happen. Hardly material for a liar.

"Don't you think that if Tano had evidence to give he wouldn't be in jail? With all respect, I don't think we can work together anymore. I'm going to continue this investigation on my own."

Roberto had never been fired from his own investigation and wasn't sure how to respond. "As you wish," he said meekly.

"No, Father. It's as you wish," she replied, irritated, and she walked briskly back to the hostel on her own.

Chapter 6

The plan for the following day was a hike in the Pyrenees. Roberto would have happily sat it out—Elio was going, so there were enough adults in the party—but his investigation had hit a wall.

Now that Enza had given him the sack, he didn't even have anyone to brainstorm ideas with. So he decided to take the day off from investigating and return to his group leader duties. A hike in the mountains might clear his mind and offer new insight.

Unfortunately, this excursion required a coach journey. The hairpin bends were painful. When they finally reached their carpark, the kids ran out of the coach full of energy and enthusiasm while Roberto tumbled out on unsteady legs and with an even more unsteady stomach.

Since being left alone in charge of the group the previous day, Lia's initial reluctance to be group leader had given way to an authoritative leadership that verged on bossiness.

"Two by two, and Roberto at the rear, checking that everyone is keeping up!" she ordered in a clarion-like voice.

Roberto was more than happy to bring up the rear. His stomach still felt like it might drop out of the soles of his sandals and he was glad to be alone for a little while.

The woods were a mixture of hazels and birches, with the occasional elder and oak over an undergrowth of ferns and ivy, with sunny patches of bracken. Everything reminded Roberto of his beloved Madonie mountains where he had grown up.

For the teens who had never left the seaside city of Palermo it was a completely new landscape. They had fun drinking from springs straight out of the rocks, crossing streams on stepping stones, and peering down burrows and holes.

After walking for a few hours, they reached a clearing with a pretty little mountain chapel and a stunning view. By now Roberto had recovered from his travel sickness and could enjoy a prayer and a picnic.

Butterflies fluttered over daisies and snapdragons, their wings like airborne petals. Teenagers capered across the meadow, challenging each other in acrobatics.

Roberto, Lia and Elio sat down together, watching the kids have fun and enjoying a picnic of baguettes freshly filled by the baker. For those few blissful hours, Roberto enjoyed the beauty of nature and didn't think about the investigation.

But when they were back on the coach and

he was in the clutches of motion sickness again, Roberto was assailed by guilt. The nausea felt like his just desert for not staying behind and doing his duty towards Tano—like Enza had done.

Roberto found her waiting for him at the hostel's door.

"I've made progress, if you're at all interested," she told him with her nose up in the air.

These words piled a little hurt pride onto the guilt. This was his case, and now someone else was making inroads without him. But there was no way to take it other than humbly.

"Can I hear what you've found out?"

"Not unless you believe that Tano is innocent."

"I'm very willing to believe it. In fact, I hope so very much."

Enza looked a little doubtful about the answer, but she decided to tell him anyway.

"While you were on your trip," she said pointedly, "I went to see him. They told me Tano wasn't allowed visitors…"

After Tano's shouting yesterday, Roberto wasn't surprised about that.

"…except for the priest, they said," Enza continued, shooting Roberto a resentful look. "But I insisted. I used all the French I could remember from school, and I told them I wouldn't leave until they let me see Tano."

"And they let you?"

"At first no, but when I told them that I wanted to see him just for a short time, not even one hour, they let me in," she said smugly.

Roberto suspected she had accidentally pronounced "hour" in a way that sounded like the ending of the French *défenseure*, and the gendarmes had mistaken her for Tano's defence lawyer.

"What did you find out?" Roberto asked eagerly.

She smiled with satisfaction at having piqued his interest. "They've found a shirt button stuck between the fingers of Mother Mary, as if she had been struggling against her kidnapper!"

"The statue must be heavy. The thief would have had to hold it against his body to carry it."

"Poor Mother Mary," Enza said with anguish.

"It's just a statue. But what does the button tell us about the thief?" Roberto asked with frustration.

"Well, none of the clothes Tano was wearing on the CCTV footage has any buttons, so it can't have come off Tano's clothes. The gendarmes asked Tano if he had any accomplices and he told them again that he had nothing to do with the statue's theft. He's very upset that they still don't believe him, but the thing that upsets him the most is that you don't believe him."

"I don't know what to believe anymore," Roberto said.

"Whatever you decide to believe, please get Tano home. I've done what I could, and I don't think the gendarmes will let me visit him again."

"I think they will," Roberto said.

"If you won't do it for him, do it for me and for his Nonna."

Tano's nonna was a good woman, who had brought him up amidst great difficulties when his parents had abandoned them both. She would hate to know that he was in jail, and in a foreign country too, where she couldn't visit him. Also, Roberto suspected, she would be appalled at this particular crime.

Chapter 7

Roberto didn't sleep that night. There was only one day left before their departure—his last chance to free Tano—and he still didn't have a plan.

He wished he hadn't chosen to have a room on his own but had shared with Giordano and Elio instead. Then he might have been able to catch the keys' thief—who might be the same as the statue's thief.

With no access to the button, no idea what it looked like and very little chance of finding its owner, he decided to go back to the only thing he had access to: the coach.

After an earnest prayer session, he left his room before anyone was up. The air was fresh with dew and smelled of herbs and butter as breakfasts were being prepared in bakeries and hotels all over town.

The coach was parked just a few hundred metres away from the hostel, in a dedicated coach parking area.

As Roberto saw a figure moving inside it, his heart jumped into his mouth. Could this be the thief who had come back to retrieve more loot?

Then the thief couldn't be Tano, because he was at the gendarmes' station! Tano might well be innocent!

Roberto sneaked up to the coach, bounded

up the steps and shouted at the intruder: "Stop where you are!"

The man jumped, yelped and turned around with his arms up like in a police movie.

"What's the matter?" Giordano asked, shaking.

"Sorry. I thought you were the statue's thief," Roberto apologised.

Giordano looked ashen.

"But it's just you," Roberto added.

"Ah, yes, just me," Giordano smiled weakly. "You gave me such a scare."

"I'm terribly sorry. I didn't think you would be up so early."

"I'm just doing my vehicle checks as I'll be driving you today while Elio takes a day off."

Roberto had a sudden idea.

"Do you check the coach every time you're about to drive it?"

"Yes. Every commercial driver should check their vehicle before driving it. It would be reckless not to."

"How do you check a vehicle?" Roberto asked.

"I start with visual checks of the outside, then the inside," Giordano said, flattered by Roberto's interest. "I check everything, from the toilets to the seatbelts to the luggage hold. Then I move on to the technical bits, like the oil level and tyre pressure," he continued, warming to the topic. "You'll have to do the same with your car when you pass your driving test—I say 'when', not 'if', because I'm sure you'll get your driving licence very soon," Giordano told him warmly.

But Roberto wasn't asking because he was interested in good vehicle maintenance practice.

"The day the statue was found in the luggage hold, you were driving the coach, so you must have done these checks that morning too, am I right?"

Giordano hesitated. "I don't remember."

"You must have done them, because you've just said that it would be reckless not to, and you are not a reckless man," Roberto pressed on.

"I don't understand where this is getting at," Giordano said, wiping his palms on his trousers.

"During your vehicle check, you would have noticed the stolen statue in the luggage hold and raised the alarm, but you didn't. The statue was only found by the gendarmes later, when they searched the coach because they suspected Tano—which you couldn't have foreseen."

Giordano took a step back.

"Tano must have put the statue in the hold after I did my checks," Giordano said, his voice trembling.

"How could he? He had already returned the keys to your room, if we are to believe the story you made up to protect yourself and pass the blame onto an easy target—someone who was already under suspicion. But Tano has nothing to do with the statue, and you know it very well. Because the one who broke the CCTV, clambered down with the statue, losing a button in the process,"—Roberto pointed at the missing button on Giordano's shirt —"and put it in the luggage hold, is you."

Giordano collapsed on one of the coach's seats and, holding his face in his hands, burst into sobs.

"Why did you do it?"

"Mother Mary didn't treat my mum very well. After all the trouble my mum went through to come here a year ago, Mother Mary didn't cure her. I thought it was only fair that this time it was Mother Mary who should take the trouble to make the journey to my mum and give her what she deserves."

"So when you heard that Father Pietro was organising a pilgrimage to Lourdes, you offered your services so that you could hide the statue in the luggage hold. Is Elio in on it too?"

"No. He doesn't know. I told him I was going to buy a replica from one of the shops, so that when he found Mother Mary in the hold he would think that it was just a replica."

Roberto didn't know where to begin his reply. Should he start with the statue being only a representation of Mary, or from the idea that miracles couldn't be extorted or earned?

In any case, this would be a long conversation, and right now, he needed to get Tano out of jail urgently.

"Are you prepared to tell the gendarmes everything, or do I have to tell them? They already have proof that it was you," Roberto said, thinking about the button.

Giordano let out another big sob. "I guess it's better if I tell them."

"I think so too."

Chapter 8

Roberto tried not to take it as a personal failure that a member of his congregation had stolen one of the most beloved objects in the Catholic world. What should worry him more, he realised, was that so many of his flock were extremely confused about the difference between the statue and the real person.

From Giordano's stunt to Lia's reaction to it, it was clear that urgent re-education was needed.

Roberto ruled out an iconoclastic rampage through the parish, not because it would cause outrage but because all the statues and paintings in their baroque church were listed. Instead, he made a mental note to read up on St Paul's preaching to the statue-worshipping pagans of Roman times.

Giordano took Tano's place in the detention cell. As the party was now travelling home with only one driver, they had to make several stops along the way to give Elio his statutory rests— which suited Roberto's stomach very well.

Giordano was sentenced to a short time in jail, of which he was grateful as it kept him out of the paparazzi's reach until the uproar had fizzled out.

Giordano's mother was extremely surprised to learn what her son had done. She had greatly enjoyed her pilgrimage to Lourdes the previous year, and had considered the trip—seeing the world and spending time with her son—a granted miracle in itself. She was utterly at peace with her disability and hadn't asked for it to be taken away from her.

Lia was still convinced that Giordano's stunt had sent Mother Mary into a sulk and had cost her father the miracle Lia had gone to Lourdes for. So she was mad at Giordano and was eagerly waiting for him to come out of jail to give him a piece of her mind.

She wasn't the only one. Tano considered himself the pinnacle of the offended parties—second only to Mother Mary—and from such dizzyingly high ground he'd forgotten that he'd been on the incriminating CCTV footage in the first place.

Instead, he went around the parish with heavy sighs and eyes rolled heavenward like the martyrs of the church's paintings, telling everyone that he had narrowly escaped the guillotine.

Roberto was ready to grovel to earn Tano's forgiveness, but he found that it wasn't needed. The young man seemed to have completely forgotten Roberto's offence, and on the coach trip back he refused again to sit with anyone else.

Enza forgave Roberto too. At the end of the trip, when the coach disgorged them all into the square in front of the church, she gave Roberto a goodbye hug.

"Father, why do you love us so much when we're not even your children?" she asked him.

Roberto hadn't expected such a profound question and thought carefully about the answer. He could tell her how, in a spiritual sense, he considered them his children too—which was why they called him "Father". He could say that he loved them because he tried to look at them through God's eyes—as flawed but beloved children. Not to forget that Jesus had told us to love each other, even our enemies.

But Enza answered for him.

"But of course, how could anyone not love Tano?"

Roberto smiled. "Quite."

The setting sun was shining softly through the church's bell towers and balusters, with a warm pink glow backlighting the curvy silhouette of the baroque church. Roberto felt that warm pink glow in his chest. He was finally home.

The End

Other books by Stefania Hartley

In this series:

Father Roberto and the Missing Money
Father Roberto and the Runaway Ring
Father Roberto and the Mystery of the
Microscope

Collections of short stories:

Tales from the Parish
Good Habits
Sweet Surprises
The Season to Be Jolly
Welcome to Quayside
Sand, Sea & Tamburello
A Season of Goodwill
To Be Loved
Drive Me Crazy
Stars Are Silver
Keeping it Cool
Fresh from the Sea
Confetti and Lemon Blossom
A Slip of the Tongue
What's Yours is Mine

Short Romances:

How to Choose a Husband
The Italian Fake Date
Sweet Competition for Camillo's Café
Second Chances at Mamma's Trattoria
Under Far Eastern Skies

ABOUT THE AUTHOR

Stefania was born in Sicily and immediately started growing, but not very much. She left her sunny island after falling head over heels in love with an Englishman, and now she lives in the UK with her husband and their three children. Having finally learnt English, she's enjoying it so much that she now writes novels and short stories which have been longlisted, shortlisted, commended, and won prizes.

If you have enjoyed these stories, please leave a review. To be the first to hear when she's releasing a new book, sign up for her newsletter and you'll receive an exclusive short story: www.stefaniahartley.com/subscribe

www.ingramcontent.com/pod-product-compliance
Lightning Source LLC
Chambersburg PA
CBHW072031170626
46811CB00008B/3024